THIRTY DAYS OF YOU

By Nessa Kallis

I0670612

Thirty Days of You
Copyright © 2025 by Georgina Horton
All rights reserved.

No part of this publication may be reproduced, distributed, or transmitted in any form or by any means, including photocopying, recording, or other electronic or mechanical methods, without the prior written permission of the publisher, except in the case of brief quotations embodied in reviews and certain other noncommercial uses permitted by copyright law.

ISBN: 979-8-9939429-8-8

For everyone who believed in new beginnings.
And for anyone who needed a reason to stay.

"Sometimes the place you're running from
is the one that's been waiting for you all along."
— Nessa Kallis

A Note from the Author

Thank you for stepping into this story with me. *Thirty Days of You* was born from a simple idea: that sometimes life gives us unexpected second chances when we least expect them.

This book is for anyone who has ever felt stuck, unsure, or afraid to start over. May Luna and West remind you that healing is rarely linear, love is rarely convenient, and new beginnings often arrive disguised as chaos.

Thank you for reading.

— Nessa Kallis

Day 30 — Luna

By the time the bus hisses to a halt at Harbor Street, the Atlantic has already climbed into my lungs and rinsed out the last ten years of Boston. I step down with my weekend suitcase and a guilt the size of a twelve-room hotel. My brain, ever helpful, starts queuing up a new playlist titled "Denial Isn't Just a River (Deluxe Edition)."

The CASTELLANO INN sign hangs crooked over peeling clapboard, a gull perched on the missing L like an impatient apostrophe. Nonna always said the building breathes. Today it wheezes as if it's been smoking for fifty years and just now decided to quit.

I take a moment before walking toward the door. In Boston, I had a life. I had deadlines and bylines and a tiny apartment that cost more per month than this entire property probably costs per year. I had friends who understood the difference between artisanal and regular coffee, who wore all black to art openings, who never asked why I wasn't married yet.

Here, I have ghosts.

The porch swing still squeaks in that particular rhythm that used to drive my father crazy. The maple tree out front has grown about two feet taller, its branches reaching toward the second-story windows like long, skeletal fingers. Everything is familiar and foreign at the same time.

The key still works, which feels like some kind of cosmic joke. The door opens to that smell - old wood, lemon polish, and something that's uniquely Nonna. Determination mixed with stubbornness and probably a hint of bourbon.

"Welcome home, sweet pea," Nonna calls from the kitchen. "I made you something terrible for dinner."

"That's my favorite kind."

The kitchen looks exactly the same - same yellow wallpaper with the tiny flowers that have been there since I was five, same crooked

4

shelf where Nonna keeps her "fancy" glasses, same table where I did my homework and cried over my first breakup and planned my escape to the big city.

Nonna is already pouring coffee before I can ask. She slides a stack of invoices across the table like surrendered flags after a battle nobody wanted to fight. Mold assessment. Roofing estimate. Plumbing emergency call that probably costs more than my entire marketing department's annual budget.

"It's worse than you told me," I say softly, already calculating how many playlists I'll need to survive this.

Nonna lifts a shoulder in that way that means "I'm old and I don't have time for your dramatics." "I did not tell you because I wanted to see your face when you fall in love again."

"Nonna."

"With the hotel, ciccia." She pats the papers like they're wayward children. "Listen to me. Summer comes fast. The season opens on June first. If we do not make the first weekend, we lose the whole summer. The bank will not wait again. Thirty days."

I cue up a mental playlist called "Optimism: The Reckoning" and hit repeat just to see if it sticks. Spoiler: it doesn't.

She holds up the fingers of one hand, decorated with rings from every decade of her life. "Trenta. We fix what must be fixed. We make it pretty. We breathe. Maybe."

Thirty days. I feel the number click into place behind my ribs like a lock turning, or maybe my anxiety finally finding a deadline to obsess over.

I set my suitcase down and take in the lobby the way I was trained to take in brand campaigns—in vignettes: the rope-wrapped banister that's been there since my grandfather installed it, the faded watercolor of fishing boats that my mother painted in high school, the bowl of sea glass I sorted by color when I was eight and insisted was "very important work."

My playlists—my ridiculous numbered playlists—begin to shuffle in my head. "Damage Control Disco." "Miracle Morning but With Saws." "Do Not Panic (Mostly Acoustic)." I consider adding "Why Did I Leave My Corporate Job Again?" but decide it's too long for a title.

"All right," I say, and my voice steadies with a confidence I absolutely do not feel. "We'll do it. We'll do whatever it takes, including but not limited to prayer, paint, and possibly a miracle or three."

"Brava." Nonna claps once, satisfied. "Kelsey said she would send coffee and a contractor."

I blink. "A what?"

"A contractor. Very serious face. Too handsome for his own peace. Probably dangerous."

My stomach does something complicated. "When?"

"This afternoon. Two o'clock." Nonna's eyes gleam with something that looks suspiciously like matchmaking. "He's very good with his hands. And very single."

I know that walk. I know the rhythm of those footsteps, the particular weight of them. I've heard them in my dreams for ten years, in the quiet moments when I let myself remember what I left behind.

"Front desk?" a voice calls—deep, unamused, somehow textured with both Manhattan and sawdust. The kind of voice that probably makes cash registers nervous.

The kind of voice I used to fall asleep listening to during movie marathons, back when we were friends who maybe wanted to be more but never quite figured out how.

I smooth my sundress and wipe my palms on my thighs, but my hands are shaking. This is fine. This is totally fine. I'm a professional adult who can handle seeing her high school almost-something after ten years of radio silence.

I turn the corner into the lobby, and there he is.

West Harding.

He's broader than I remember, as if the years have added muscle and maybe some armor. Dark hair, a day of scruff that should be illegal, work belt hugging lean hips, sun-browned forearms marked by silver threads of old cuts that probably have interesting stories. But it's his eyes that stop me—storm-gray and guarded, taking in everything and giving nothing back.

Those eyes find mine, and the world tilts.

For a moment—just a heartbeat—something flickers across his face. Recognition. Surprise. Something that might be pain or might be hope or might be both tangled together like the wires in Room Four.

Then it's gone, replaced by that careful neutrality I remember from senior year, from the night before I left for Boston, from every moment when we almost said something real but didn't.

Beside him, a German Shepherd mix sits like a prince who knows he is loved and has excellent taste in humans. The dog's tail starts wagging the moment he sees me, like he knows something his owner won't admit.

"Luna." My name in his mouth sounds different than it did ten years ago. Rougher. More careful. As if he's testing the weight of it.

"West." I try to smile, but my face feels frozen. "Hi."

"Hi." He shifts his weight, and I notice he's gripping his notebook a little too tightly. "Kelsey said you needed help with the inn."

"Yeah. Yes. We do." I'm babbling. I never babble. "It's—well, you can see. It's a disaster."

"I've seen worse." His voice is steady, professional, but there's something underneath it that makes my chest ache. "Kelsey mentioned you were back in town."

Of course she did. Kelsey, my best friend since kindergarten, who knew exactly what she was doing when she recommended West for this job. Who probably orchestrated this entire thing with Nonna because they're both incurable romantics who think ten years of silence can be fixed with proximity and power tools.

"Just for thirty days," I say quickly, like I need him to know I'm not staying, and I need to protect both of us from whatever this is. "To help Nonna get the inn ready for summer."

"Right." Something in his jaw tightens. "Thirty days."

The silence stretches between us, heavy with all the things we didn't say ten years ago. With the goodbye I never gave him. With the letters I wrote but never sent. With the way I used to draw tiny hearts in the margins of my chemistry notes and hope he'd notice.

"This is Moose," West says finally, gesturing to the dog, who has abandoned all pretense of dignity and is now wagging his entire body at me.

"Moose." I crouch down, grateful for the excuse to break eye contact, and the dog immediately leans into my hand like we're old friends. "Hey, buddy. You're a good boy, aren't you?"

Moose makes a sound that's half-whine, half-agreement, and I feel West's eyes on me. When I look up, he's watching us with an expression I can't quite read.

"He likes you," West says quietly.

"I like him too." I stand up, brushing dog hair off my sundress, trying to find my footing in this conversation. "So. The inn. Should we—do you want to see what we're working with?"

"Yeah." He pulls out his notebook, all business now. "Let's start with the basics. What's the timeline?"

"Thirty days," I repeat, and the number feels different now. Not like a countdown to freedom, but like a ticking clock on something I'm not ready to name. "We need eight rooms and two suites guest-ready. The restaurant can be scaled back to breakfast and small plates. The roof deck is non-negotiable."

His mouth does that micro-twitch I remember from chemistry class, when Mr. Peterson would assign impossible problem sets and West would already be calculating solutions in his head.

"Non-negotiable roof decks are how budgets bleed out and contractors develop ulcers."

"It's where couples fall in love," I say before I can stop myself, and immediately want to take it back because of course that's what I would say. Of course I would make this awkward.

He glances at me—one sharp, assessing look that feels like it's seeing straight through all my carefully constructed walls. "Right."

The word hangs between us, loaded with memory. The roof deck is where we used to study together, back when studying was an excuse to be near each other. Where we watched the sunset on the last day of senior year and almost—almost—said something real.

Where I should have told him I was leaving. Where I should have asked him to wait for me.

Where I didn't.

"Budget?" he asks, flipping a page, and I'm grateful he's letting it go.

I tell him. He exhales through his nose like he's trying not to say something that will make me cry.

"You're optimistic," he says, which is definitely code for "you're delusional."

"I'm determined," I correct, falling into the old rhythm of our banter like no time has passed at all. "There's a difference. Optimism is for people who haven't seen the plumbing invoice yet."

The corner of his mouth twitches—not quite a smile, but close. "Fair enough."

We do the walk-through, and it's torture. Not because of the inn's condition, though that's bad enough. But because West moves through the space with that same quiet competence I remember, testing things with steady hands, making notes in his careful handwriting, offering Moose exactly one quiet knuckle rub every time the dog checks in.

Because being near him feels like coming home and running away at the same time.

Because every room holds a memory I've been trying to forget: the breakfast nook where he helped me study for the SATs, the honeymoon suite where we hid during my cousin's wedding reception and talked until dawn, the roof deck where everything almost changed.

"The plumbing's creative," he says when we're back in the lobby, and I can hear the diplomatic restraint in his voice. "We can reroute with PEX. Faster, cheaper. Won't be pretty behind the walls, but it'll work."

"Do it." I'm trying to sound professional, but my voice comes out softer than I intended. "Whatever it takes."

He looks at me then—really looks at me—and for a moment the careful neutrality slips. "Luna—"

"Coffee?" Nonna appears as though she's been waiting for her cue, already pouring like caffeine is the answer to everything. Which, to be fair, it usually is.

West takes the cup, and I watch his hands—the same hands that used to help me with calculus homework, that built a bookshelf for my dorm room the week before I left, that almost reached for mine a hundred times but never quite did.

"This is... strong," he says after a sip, and I almost laugh because some things never change.

"It is honest," Nonna says, looking between us with eyes that see too much. "Like you both should be."

The silence that follows is deafening.

"I should show you the office," I say quickly, desperate to escape whatever Nonna is trying to orchestrate. "The invoices, the timeline, all the fun stuff."

West follows me, Moose trailing behind like a furry chaperone. In the office, I spread out the papers—the evidence of everything that's broken, everything that needs fixing.

"It's a lot," I admit, and I'm not just talking about the inn anymore.

"It is." He studies the invoices with that focused intensity I remember, the one that used to make my heart do stupid things. "But it's doable. If we work together."

Together. The word sits between us like a promise and a threat.

"West," I start, then stop, because I don't know what I'm trying to say. I'm sorry? I missed you? I think about you every time I hear that stupid song we used to listen to?

"Tomorrow," he says, saving me from myself. "Seven a.m. We start with demolition."

"Tomorrow," I repeat, and it feels like we're agreeing to more than just a work schedule.

He reaches the threshold and stops. Looks back. And for a second, I see it—the boy I knew, the one who used to look at me as if I was the answer to a question he was afraid to ask.

"It's good to see you, Luna," he says quietly. "Even if it's complicated."

Then he's gone, Moose flowing after him like a furry shadow, and I'm left standing in the lobby of my grandmother's inn, heart racing, hands shaking, playlist already forming in my head.

"That went well," Nonna says from behind me, and I jump.

"Nonna! How long have you been standing there?"

"Long enough." She taps her cane against the floor, satisfied. "He still looks at you the same way."

"What way?"

"Like you are the ocean and he is drowning, but he does not want to be saved."

I sink onto the lobby couch, suddenly exhausted. "I left without saying goodbye."

"I know." Nonna sits beside me, her hand finding mine. "And now you are back. So say hello properly this time."

"It's been ten years, Nonna. He probably hates me."

"That boy does not hate you." She squeezes my hand. "He is hurt, yes. Angry, maybe. But hate? No. Hate is easy. What he feels is much more complicated."

I think about the way he looked at me in the office. The careful distance he maintained. The moment on the threshold when his guard slipped.

"I don't know if I can do this," I whisper.

"Do what? Fix the inn or fix your heart?"

"Both. Either. I don't know."

Nonna stands, leaning on her cane. "Then you make a playlist, yes? That is what you do when things are complicated. You make a playlist and you figure it out one song at a time."

She's right. She's always right.

After a simple dinner of Nonna's "terrible" cooking (which is actually delicious pasta carbonara), I find myself restless. The house is quiet, and the only sounds are the creaks of an old building settling into itself. My old bedroom feels too small, too full of memories. I pull on a sweatshirt and slip outside for an evening walk, drawn to the property in the moonlight.

The inn has always been my favorite place in the world, even when I was desperate to leave it. There's magic in these walls, in the way the moonlight hits the windows, in the stories embedded in every floorboard.

I find myself at the back of the property, near the old carriage house that's been falling apart for as long as I can remember. The door is partially open, swinging slightly in the breeze. I shouldn't go in - it's probably full of spiders and structural instability and things that bite.

But I do anyway.

The inside is exactly what you'd expect: dusty, forgotten, filled with old furniture that's been slowly rotting for decades. But there's something else here too - something that feels important. I run my hand along the wall, and my fingers catch on something loose.

A small, loose stone in the foundation. I pull it out, and behind it is a small metal box.

Not just any box. This is my mother's handwriting on the label. For Luna. When you're ready.

My heart stops. My mother died when I was twelve, and this is the first thing I've found of hers in years. The last thing I found was her recipe box, which Nonna keeps but never lets me touch.

I open the box carefully. Inside are letters, dozens of them, each addressed to me. For when you turn sixteen. For when you fall in love. For when you have your heart broken. For when you need to come home.

The last one is labeled simply, For when you remember.

I sink to the floor of the dusty carriage house, letters in my lap, moonlight streaming through the broken windows, and realize that maybe I haven't come back to The Castellano Inn by accident at all.

Maybe this is exactly where I'm supposed to be.

Later, I carry the letters back to my room and tuck them safely in my nightstand drawer. I'm not ready to read them yet—not tonight, not after everything that's happened today. But knowing they're there, knowing my mother left me these pieces of herself, makes something in my chest ease a little.

That night, I sit on the edge of the honeymoon suite tub with a lemon-scented scrub brush and scrub until the porcelain remembers it is supposed to shine. Out the window the ocean breathes in and out, in and out, counting for me. Thirty days.

Thirty days to fix the inn.

Thirty days to figure out what I want.

Thirty days to decide if I'm brave enough to say the things I should have said ten years ago.

I make a new playlist and name it "Demolition Therapy (Emotional Edition)." Tomorrow, we tear down the wrong walls and maybe build some right ones.

Tomorrow, I face West Harding again and all the feelings I've been running from.

Tomorrow, everything changes.

Today's Playlist:

"Denial Isn't Just a River (Deluxe Edition)" – Anxiety in A Minor

"Optimism: The Reckoning" – Hope in C Major

"Demolition Therapy (Emotional Edition)" – Begin Again, But With Feelings This Time

Day 29 — West

Ten years. It's been ten years since Luna Castellano packed her bags and left this town without so much as a goodbye. Ten years since I've seen her face except in the occasional photo Nonna still keeps on her mantel.

And now she's back.

I got the call from Nonna two days ago. "Luna's coming home, West. And we need your help with the inn."

I almost said no. Almost told her I was too busy, that I had other jobs lined up, that I couldn't possibly take on another major renovation project. But I heard the hope in Nonna's voice, and besides, I'm not that good at lying to myself.

Drywall dust: the confetti of poor life choices. I believe coffee is a moral compass. Bad brew, bad day. It's also a personality test—mine says "sarcasm with a chance of redemption." Harbor Street may be loud, but bad coffee is louder. If the first sip tastes like despair, you can assume the day will follow suit. I make a mental note to buy beans that don't taste like someone whispered "espresso" near a cup of hot water.

Harbor Street is already awake when Moose and I roll the truck up to the curb—gulls heckling like they're auditioning for a nature documentary, boat engines grumbling like they need coffee too, somebody's wind chimes arguing with the breeze about which one is more annoying. I kill the ignition and listen to the building. Old places talk. This one mutters like a conspiracy theorist who knows things about you.

The job board at Miller's Hardware had said it all: "Wanted: Contractor for Castellano Inn Renovation. Must be patient, reasonably priced, and immune to Nonna's matchmaking attempts. References required. Bring coffee."

I found myself staring at that note for a solid five minutes, trying to decide if this was the universe giving me a second chance or just

15

setting me up for another round of heartache. Then Nonna called, and as always, I didn't stand a chance.

Moose noses my elbow. "Yeah, yeah. I see you." He knows the drill—first walk-through, then water, then he steals someone's heart with those eyes that should be illegal. The dog's got game, I'll give him that.

But today is different. Today, when I walk into the inn, she'll be there. Luna. The girl who sat behind me in chemistry and drew tiny hearts in the margins of her notebook. The girl who helped me study for finals and fell asleep on my shoulder during movie marathons. The girl who left without saying goodbye and took half my heart with her.

I take a deep breath and grab my tool belt. Time to face my past and hope I don't mess up the future.

Inside, Luna's got a folding table set up like a command center for an invasion: floor plans that look like treasure maps, a box of contractor bags that probably cost more than my first truck, a tray of muffins that look illegal in twelve different states, and a speaker pulsing something bright that shouldn't work at seven a.m. but does anyway. She's wearing cutoffs and a T-shirt with paint on the hem and optimism on her mouth like it's a new shade of lipstick.

She holds up a travel mug as a peace offering or possibly a test. "Coffee," she says. "Allegedly drinkable."

I take it. It's good—too good. "You bribing me?"

"I'm incentivizing excellence," she says, as if that's a normal thing to say before sunrise.

"Noted." I hand her a respirator mask. "You wearing this. Non-negotiable. I don't want your grandmother haunting me because you inhaled asbestos."

She salutes with the elastic like she's joining the army of proper safety procedures. "Sir, yes, sir."

We suit up. I lay out the day: demo walls in rooms two and four, pull the cracked tile in the honeymoon bath, check joists for rot, cap the worst pipes, haul out debris by noon if the dump runs fast and the universe is feeling generous.

She listens like a student planning to ace the final and bake the professor cookies to seal the deal. It should annoy me. It doesn't. It's... distracting. Moose chooses Luna duty without asking. He stations himself at her boots like he's her personal bodyguard, which is fine except he's supposed to be my foreman. Traitor.

"Ready?" I ask, trying to sound like a guy who has his life together.

She cranks her playlist. The first track is some 80s anthem that makes the building square its shoulders like it's getting ready for a fight. "Ready."

The crowbar bites. The first sheet of drywall peels back with a sound like rain and secrets and twenty years of questionable decisions. Dust blooms; sunlight catches it and turns the air into glitter you shouldn't inhale but want to anyway. Luna's eyes are wide above the mask, and when she swings—awkward at first, then with rhythm like she's been practicing in her sleep—something opens in her posture. People either flinch at destruction or find religion in it. She's the second kind, and it's unnervingly attractive.

We work. Hours become the clean math of effort. Sweat, pry, haul, repeat. She learns fast—how to angle the bar to save her wrist, how to read the shadow of a stud, how to listen for hollow versus solid like she's developing some kind of construction ESP. We stack debris, bag insulation, curse at a nest of wires that someone in 1978 called "good enough" which is basically a historical war crime against electrical systems.

By ten, she's humming. By noon, the room is a ribcage of exposed studs and possibilities. I like bones. Bones tell the truth. They don't lie about being level or having good intentions.

Nonna appears with sandwiches and judgments. She tries to hand-feed Moose prosciutto like he's royalty. He pretends to resist for half a second, then sells his integrity for meat like a common criminal. I've never been so disappointed in him.

"You work too quiet," Nonna tells me, like being quiet is a crime. "Men who are loud are lazy. But men who are too quiet are thinking of leaving."

"Nonna," Luna warns, cheeks flushed. She looks good flushed. I aim my eyes at a joist like my life depends on it and mentally recite the periodic table.

"I'm thinking of load-bearing," I say, which is technically true.

"Bene," Nonna says, not believing me for a second. She taps a beam like she's blessing it. "Make this one strong. It knows things."

After lunch I crawl under the honeymoon suite to confirm what I already know: the plumbing's a fairy tale told by a drunk uncle who doesn't understand physics. I come back with cobwebs in my hair and a theory that makes me want to retire and move to a desert.

"Bad?" Luna asks.

"Creative," I say, which is the nicest word I can come up with. I sketch in the dust on the floor like I'm drawing ancient runes. "We can reroute with PEX. Faster, cheaper. It won't be pretty behind the walls, but it'll work. Probably."

She studies my drawing like it's choreography and she's already hearing the music. "Do it."

"You sure? It means the tub stays. Resurfaced, not replaced."

She looks at the stained porcelain like it personally offended her mother, then she exhales like she's making peace with her enemy. "The tub has history. I'll make it shine."

Something tight in my chest lets go a fraction. People who save the right things are rare. Most people tear down everything that doesn't sparkle immediately.

By late afternoon we've filled the dumpster and cleared the worst of the rot. Luna's sitting cross-legged on the drop cloth, pulling nails and sorting them into a jar she's labeled "Our Bad Choices." Moose has adopted the jar as a personal security issue and stares at it like it might hatch.

"You always label your jars?" I ask, because I'm a glutton for conversational punishment.

"Only the important ones," she says, tucking a loose strand behind her ear, leaving a clean line of dust on her temple that I want to wipe away but don't. "I make playlists, too."

"So I heard." I've heard them for two days straight. They're growing on me like mold.

She brightens like I've just given her a puppy. "Do you want one?"

"For demo days?" I ask, like there's such a thing as demo-specific music.

"For moods. I have 'Do Not Panic (Mostly Acoustic).' Also 'What If We Just Try' which sounds suspiciously like emotional gambling."

"I'm more of a silence-and-podcasts guy," I say, because silence is safer.

She points at my coffee cup like she's caught me in a lie. "You're also a liar. You like this song."

I don't. Then the chorus hits and my foot taps. Fine. I do. "It's... tolerable."

She grins, and something in the room tilts toward light like a sunflower following the sun. This is getting dangerous.

We call it at six. My shoulders ache in the honest way that means I've actually worked for a living. Luna stands in the doorway of the honeymoon suite and looks at the mess like it's a map only she can read, like she sees the future in the destruction.

"This is going to be beautiful," she says softly, and I almost believe her.

"If we don't die from mold exposure first," I say, because someone has to be the voice of reason. "Your enthusiasm is inspiring, if slightly concerning."

"I try," she says, laughing that unguarded kind that sneaks under fences and steals your socks when you're not looking. Moose goes to her like a tide that's found its favorite shore. She drops a hand to his head without looking, like they've been doing this dance forever. It's... coordinated. Like they rehearsed being soft together when I wasn't watching.

I gather my tools. She gathers courage. "Thank you," she says. "For not running."

I shrug, because admitting that I thought about it feels too vulnerable. "It's a job."

Her smile thins, and I hate that I notice, hate that I caused it, hate that I care. "Right. Well—tomorrow we paint?"

"Tomorrow we find what else the walls lied about," I say, gesturing to the exposed pipes that look like metal spaghetti. "Then we paint."

She nods. "I'll bring muffins. And the 'Demolition Therapy' playlist."

Moose betrays me one more time by whining when we head for the door. "You live here now?" I ask him, like he owes me loyalty.

He thumps his tail against Luna's shin like he's signing a lease and changing his address without consulting me.

"Traitor," I tell him.

He smiles with his whole body, the unapologetic mutt.

Outside, the sky is a bruise healing toward lavender. I load the truck while trying not to look at Luna through the window, trying not to think about her laugh or the way she touched the worst part of the hotel like it was deserving of love. I put on a murder podcast to rinse my head of sweetness, but it's not working. Moose sighs and sticks his nose in the wind like he's trying to catch her scent.

The episode is about a contractor who ignored a hairline crack and the disastrous metaphor that followed. "Not today," I tell the steering wheel. "We're not cracking."

I consider stopping for coffee that doesn't taste like existential regret, then remember the last café gave me grounds that looked like they'd survived an apocalypse. Moose sneezes like he disagrees with my life choices.

When I park at my rental, my phone buzzes. Seattle. The job I told myself I needed to want. I watch it ring until it stops, feeling like I just dodged a bullet I can't explain.

"Thirty days," I tell Moose. "I'll give them thirty."

Moose leans his head on my knee like an oath, like he understands promises made to the universe at dusk. Tomorrow, we start putting bones back together.

Today's Playlist:

"Moral Compass Malfunction" – Sarcasm in B Flat

"Deconstruction Nation" – Heavy Metal Demo Day

"Traitor Dog, Loyal Heart" – Acoustic Guilt Trip

Day 28 — Luna

The morning smells like salt and sawdust and the kind of hope that should probably come with a warning label. It's giving DIY montage energy—minus the budget, coordinated flannel outfits, and the magical ability to paint a whole room in thirty seconds. Somewhere, a rom com audience is screaming for a meet cute that's already in progress but refuses to follow the script.

I didn't know salt and sawdust could belong together, but now they do, like two people who shouldn't work but somehow make each other better.

By eight a.m. the inn is alive—hammer thuds creating percussion for the morning symphony, Moose snoring between toolboxes like he's conducting a nap orchestra, Nonna humming opera somewhere in the kitchen like she's personally coaching the sun to rise faster. West moves through the chaos like gravity in a T-shirt, calm and constant and entirely too distracting for this early in the morning.

I hover with a paintbrush I don't yet deserve to use, feeling like an imposter at a home renovation convention.

He glances at me, one eyebrow doing that thing that makes my stomach do a tiny flip. "You planning to paint the air, or the wall?"

"I'm waiting for inspiration," I say, like that's a legitimate construction strategy.

"Or permission?" he asks, because apparently he can read my mind and it's annoyingly attractive.

I meet his eyes, trying for confidence and ending up somewhere between flustered and determined. "I don't ask for that anymore."

He looks away first, which I'm counting as a small victory in the war against emotional walls that are taller than the ones we're literally building.

We've fallen into a rhythm already: I handle the cosmetic; he handles the structural. Somewhere in the overlap, we keep bumping

22

into each other like sentences that won't punctuate, like two people who are sharing oxygen and pretending not to notice. When the light hits right, the dust turns to glitter again, and I pretend I'm not watching the way it catches in his hair.

I tape edges with a precision that would impress my old marketing director and key up my new playlist: "Primer + Hope." West mutters at a stubborn valve like it's personally offended him; I whisper encouragement to a wall that definitely needs therapy. We are both ridiculous and both entirely serious, and I'm starting to think this might be what happiness feels like.

My internal narrator adds: If HGTV saw us, they'd call this episode "Flirtation and Foundation Damage," which honestly sounds like a much better show than half the stuff they actually air.

"Question," I say, climbing a ladder to reach the crown molding in Room Two. "If the building breathes, do we owe it yoga?"

"Ventilation," he says without looking up, like he's been preparing for this exact question his whole life. "But sure. Downward dog for the HVAC."

"Ha. Dog." I grin at Moose, who has assumed the exact position like he's been practicing yoga in secret and is finally showing off his skills.

An hour in, the radio silence between us starts to feel like something earned rather than awkward. I paint; he re-routes plumbing with the quiet intensity of a surgeon who's operating on someone he secretly cares about. When he drills, I count the beats and fill the gaps with brushstrokes. He's a metronome I refuse to admit I like, but my playlists keep getting softer around him, and I'm not sure what that means.

"Lunch," Nonna declares at noon, appearing with caprese sandwiches and the reminder that hydration is a sacrament and dehydration is a sin. She sets a glass in front of West, then another, then another, like she's building a small fortress of water around him in case he tries to escape.

"You will not faint," she warns, like she's seen things.

"I don't faint," West says, with the dignity of someone who's definitely never fainted but maybe thought about it once during a particularly boring meeting.

"You will not faint," she repeats, satisfied when he downs one in three swallows like he's afraid she'll make him drink more if he doesn't comply.

We eat on the back steps where the breeze feels like forgiveness and the ocean sounds like it's telling secrets. Moose patrols for tomato slices like they're contraband. West keeps his shoulders angled toward the door like he's ready to go back to work mid-chew, like he's afraid of stillness.

"Why here?" he asks finally, nodding at the inn, the water, my ridiculous heart that's currently doing interpretive dance behind my ribs. "You could have stayed in Boston. Had a real job. Normal hours."

"Because it's ours," I say, and the word comes out more fiercely than I intended. "And because it remembers me. Boston was... something I was trying on. This fits. This feels like coming home to myself."

He considers that, like he's turning the words over in his mind and finding them more complicated than expected. "Takes nerve to pick what fits."

"Takes nerve to leave what doesn't," I say, and he doesn't flinch, but something in his jaw loosens like a knot I didn't know was there.

After lunch, I tackle the Wall That Eats Light in Room Four. I peel back a layer of brittle wallpaper and find another beneath it—green ivy from the nineties that probably seemed like a good idea at the time—then another, floral from the seventies that looks like it survived a disco apocalypse. Generations of decisions, one over the other, like a family tree of questionable taste.

I run my fingers over a corner and feel letters gouged into the plaster. "West," I call. "Come see."

He wipes his hands on his jeans and joins me, his presence somehow making the dusty room feel smaller and more intimate. I angle the work lamp. There, faint but insistent: R + E 1976.

"Romeo and... Ethel?" I offer, because sometimes you have to break tension with terrible suggestions.

"Ralph and Edna," he deadpans, and I nearly drop the lamp because he made a joke.

"Reckless and Everything," I say, softer than I meant to, because suddenly these initials feel like they're telling our story too.

He taps the initials, the pad of his finger gentle against the plaster, gentle against time. "Keep it."

"Can we?" I ask, because I'm afraid of wanting too much.

"We'll patch around it. Clear coat. Let it show." His voice lowers like he's sharing a secret. "Some bones deserve to be seen."

I swallow against the lump in my throat. "Okay."

We frame the relic like we're building a tiny museum, like we're honoring a love story that happened before we were born. It feels like a quiet promise: not everything old needs to be erased to make room for what's next. Some things are worth preserving, worth building around, worth making space for.

By late afternoon, the honeymoon bath is a battlefield of removed tile and hopeful lists. I'm on my knees with a grout saw when my phone pings. Kelsey: Emergency latte run? Contractor still alive? Also, Brenda wants to know if Moose is single.

I text back a photo of West's scowl and Moose's smile and she replies with seventeen heart-eyes and one skull, which feels like an accurate representation of my current emotional state.

"Don't post me," West says without looking up, like he has some kind of social media radar.

I freeze, caught. "I wouldn't."

He glances over, reads the truth on my face, and nods. "Thanks."

Sunset burns the windows coral and gold, painting the room in colors that feel like promises. We clean brushes in companionable silence, the kind that feels earned after a day of hard work and unspoken things. Nonna waves goodnight and threatens to haunt anyone who tracks dust into her kitchen after ten, which honestly seems fair.

Moose chooses a corner and makes it holy with snoring, his tail twitching like he's chasing dream squirrels. I'm wiping the last streak from the breakfast nook window when West's reflection appears next to mine in the glass.

"You're good at this," he says, and his voice is softer than I've heard it.

"At what?" I ask, though I think I know.

"Staying."

I don't know what to do with the warmth that puts in my chest, so I cap the paint and label the can "Room Two — Summer White, Brighter Than My Doubts." Then I add in smaller letters: "Also Good At Avoiding Emotional Conversations."

"Tomorrow?" I ask, because asking about anything else feels too dangerous.

"Tomorrow," he says. "Seven."

He gathers his tools. I gather my courage again. When he reaches the door, Moose hesitates and looks between us like a child of divorce who can't decide which parent has the better snacks.

"Go on," I tell the dog. "Your dad needs you."

West huffs a laugh, and it's the closest thing to a real laugh I've heard from him. "He's not wrong."

"Goodnight, Moose," I say, scratching behind his ear. "Guard the serious face."

The door clicks shut. The inn exhales around me like it's been holding its breath too. I put on a quiet song and stand in the center of the lobby until the melody tells me I've done enough for today, until it tells me that maybe, just maybe, I'm doing something right.

Today's Playlist:

"DIY Montage Energy" – Construction Pop Anthem

"Flirtation and Foundation Damage" – Acoustic Tension

"What If We Just Try" – Hope in Progress

Day 27 — West

I have a rule: if the day starts before my second cup of coffee, it's already suspicious. This morning smells like salt, lemon cleaner, and emotional risk—all of which I tolerate better with caffeine. Moose watches me work like he's my supervisor, which would be fine if he did anything besides sigh dramatically and judge my life choices. I tell him, "You're really earning that nap schedule," but he just blinks, unrepentant, like a tiny furry tyrant who knows he's cute and uses it as a weapon.

Above me, Luna starts singing off-key to something that might once have been Motown but has been thoroughly murdered by enthusiasm. I smirk and think, This must be what enlightenment sounds like to people with bad taste. Then I realize I'm smiling and blame the caffeine, even though we both know it's a lie.

The trick with old pipe is not to take it personally when it breaks in your hands. The trick with new feelings is the same. I'm not sure when my life became a plumbing metaphor, but here we are.

I'm under the honeymoon suite at eight with a headlamp, a PEX cutter, and a prayer I don't say out loud because I'm pretty sure God is busy with actual important things and doesn't need to hear about my inability to maintain emotional boundaries. Above me, Luna is still singing that Motown-atrocity, and Moose keeps crawling to the edge of the access hatch to check I haven't fallen into the earth or been kidnapped by raccoons.

"Back, foreman," I tell him. He sighs and obeys, but not before giving me a look that says "I'm only doing this because she fed me earlier."

By ten, the new lines are flirting with straight and the pressure test passes without drama, which feels like a minor miracle considering the state of everything else in this building. I give the joists a last, appreciative pat and crawl out into daylight, feeling like I've emerged from the underworld or possibly a very dirty spa treatment.

28

Luna's on her knees at the tub, sleeves pushed up, lemon cleaner making the room smell like a polished memory. The porcelain already reflects more light than it did yesterday, like it's remembering how to be beautiful again.

"Told you it would shine," she says without looking up, like she knew I was watching her.

"You did," I admit, and I hate how much I like being wrong around her, how much I like the way she looks when she's proving herself right.

We eat standing up—her, an apple with aggressive convictions that should probably be registered as a weapon; me, a protein bar that tastes like regret and cardboard—while we walk through the afternoon plan. Electrical check. Patch hallway. Pick a trim color. The kind of mundane tasks that feel important when you're doing them together.

"Not white," she says, when I suggest the obvious choice.

"White is what you pick when you're scared."

"Sometimes white is what you pick when the building is small and the ocean is big," I counter, pointing at a strip of molding that needs to be replaced. "Try a warm gray. Calm without pretending to be exciting."

She considers this, tilting her head like she's actually thinking about it. "You're secretly poetic."

"I'm openly practical," I say, because admitting anything else feels dangerous.

Kelsey swings in at noon with coffee and a machine-gun summary of town gossip that I'm pretty sure includes information about at least three people I've never met. She kisses Luna's cheek, scratches Moose like he's royalty, and tries to read me like a receipt I didn't want.

"So you must be West," she says. "The one with the murder podcasts and the scowl."

"Sometimes they're documentaries," I say, because I feel the need to defend my audio choices.

"Mm-hmm." She eyes Luna, then me, then the orbit between us where we pretend gravity isn't a factor and we're not slowly being pulled toward each other like planets. "I'm making dinner tonight. You should both come by after you're done pretending you're not in love with this building."

Luna chokes on foam. "We're... working."

"Exactly," Kelsey says, as if she's given us permission we didn't need and will take anyway. "Six." She points at me. "No scowling at my gnocchi. They're sensitive."

She is gone in a tornado of bells and roasted coffee air before either of us can protest again, leaving behind the scent of chaos and the distinct feeling that we've just been ambushed by social obligations.

"Do you—" Luna starts.

"I have plans," I say too fast, then hear the lie ring in the air like a badly tuned guitar and add, "Paperwork." Which is also a lie, but sounds more responsible.

"Paperwork is a plan," she says lightly, but the disappointed way she smooths it into fine makes my molars ache. It's the kind of polite disappointment that's worse than anger.

In the afternoon, the inn tests us. A hidden junction box plays dead. A patch feathers badly. I mismeasure a cut by an inch and say a word my father would have grounded me for using in the house. Luna doesn't flinch; she recalculates the molding run and saves my pride without calling it that, without making me feel stupid for the mistake.

By five, we've won enough small battles to call the day even. The building creaks in a language I'm starting to understand: you showed up; I will meet you halfway. I load the last of the debris while Luna locks the front desk drawer with the theatrical solemnity of a ship captain sealing the log for a journey that's changing course.

Kelsey's invitation sits between us on the lobby table like a dare, like a test I'm not sure I want to take.

"Go," I tell Luna, because someone should get to have normal social interactions, and it's clearly not going to be me. "You should eat something someone else makes for you. Someone who doesn't think salt is optional and protein bars are food groups."

"You should, too," she says, and there's hope in her voice that I can't bear to crush.

"I don't—" The words stick to old glue in my throat, to memories of Seattle and dinners that felt more like interviews than meals. Want to be seen. Know how to be new in a small town. Trust my appetite for comfort. "Maybe next time."

"Okay," she says, and the okay is careful, like she's handling something fragile.

Moose, of course, mutinies. At the door he plants his butt and refuses to move, looking between us like a child of divorce who can't decide which parent has the better snacks and which one is more likely to let him sleep on the furniture.

He looks at Luna. He looks at me. He looks at the inn like he'd like to file for joint custody of all of us.

"Come on," I coax. "I feed you."

He stays.

"I will name the next playlist after you."

He stays but wags, because he's a traitor but also negotiable.

"Coward," Luna tells him affectionately. "You just like my shampoo."

"He's a traitor," I confirm, then add, "We can walk you over. I'll pick him up there."

We cross Harbor Street together in the blue hour, the air tasting like salt and something sweet from Kelsey's kitchen. Luna walks with her shoulders back like someone who learned the weight of duty and decided to carry it anyway, like someone who's stronger than she knows. Moose paces between us, switching loyalties every three steps like he's playing emotional ping-pong.

Kelsey's place is warm-lighted and loud with a pan sizzling. She greets Luna with a spoon, me with a squint, and Moose with devotion that frankly hurts my feelings.

"You made it," she says. "I'm proud of your life choices. Even the ones that involve denying yourself homemade gnocchi."

"I can't stay," I say, like a broken record.

"Everyone says that," she replies, already setting a plate like she knows exactly how this story ends. "Then they do."

I should leave. I don't. The gnocchi is unreasonable. The conversation is easier than it has any right to be. I learn that Luna once organized the pantry at the inn by cereal box height and then documented it on a spreadsheet, which is somehow both hilarious and exactly what I would expect from her. She learns that I once rebuilt a porch with a neighbor using nothing but salvage and stubbornness. Kelsey learns that Moose will sit for parmesan but only if it's freshly grated.

After dinner, I stand to go three different times and get ambushed by more stories, more laughter, more of the easy warmth that I've been avoiding like it's contagious. When I finally make it to the door, Luna walks me out, and the street is quiet, the moon throwing a path across the water as if offering directions back to where I keep insisting I'm not going.

"Thank you," she says, and it sounds like for the pipes, the patch, the not leaving, the leaving anyway. For all of it.

"Good food," I say, because I am a coward of the ordinary sort, because saying anything else feels too big.

"Good day," she counters. "Could've been worse."

"No one died," I allow, which is my version of glowing praise.

"High bar," she says, smiling.

"Tomorrow, seven?" I ask, because routine is safer than feelings.

"Tomorrow," she says, and this time it feels like a promise we both heard.

Back at my rental, Seattle calls again. I let it go to voicemail I won't check. Moose drops his head on my thigh and exhales the kind of trust I don't deserve yet, the kind of trust that feels heavier than any tool I carry.

I open my notebook and rewrite tomorrow's list twice, as if organization could make me immune to the shape of her laugh, to the way she looks when she's passionate about something, to the fact that I'm in way over my head and don't want to be saved.

I put on a symphony so the strings can say the things I won't. Moose snores in time. Outside, the ocean keeps its own playlist and refuses to turn it down.

Thirty days left. The building is not the only thing under renovation.

Today's Playlist:
"Emotional Risk Assessment" – Caffeinated Anxiety
"Plumbing Metaphors for Feelings" – Pipe Dreams in D Minor
"The Building Speaks" – Structural Integrity Blues

Day 26 — Luna

The sound of rain on the roof wakes me before sunrise. It isn't polite rain—it's loud and full of opinions, drumming against the old shingles like applause from the heavens or possibly like the universe is trying to tell me something but refuses to use indoor voices. I curl deeper into my blanket, listening to the building hum beneath the storm, wondering if rain has different accents in different places.

When I finally pad downstairs, West is already there, soaked to the elbows, holding a tarp like a knight holding a defeated flag after a battle he won but doesn't look happy about winning.

"Morning," I say, offering a towel like I'm some kind of medieval lady-in-waiting to his damp knightliness.

"Roof leak," he says, shaking his hair out like a dog, which is ironic given his actual dog is currently giving me side-eye from the corner like I'm interrupting important business. "North corner. Temporary fix bought us twelve hours. We'll need new shingles."

"Twelve hours buys us breakfast," I offer. "Coffee's hot. Nonna's been up since dawn making something that smells like heaven and possibly judgment."

He eyes the mug warily, as if it contains emotional commitment or poison or both. "You first."

I take a sip and raise an eyebrow. "See? Not poison. Just coffee. Although Nonna did say something about putting love in it, which could be code for anything."

He takes it, mutters something about caffeine diplomacy, and drinks. The storm rumbles approval like it's in on the joke.

Moose sits by the window, watching rain slide down the glass with the intensity of someone watching a boring nature documentary.

Nonna hums in the kitchen, making frittata like it's a weapon against chaos and possibly against my terrible life choices. "Today," West says, all business like he's trying to build a wall between us with

34

words, "we patch what we can. I'll check attic beams after the rain. You should take inventory—paint, supplies, anything we need before the weekend."

"Bossy," I tease, because teasing him is becoming my favorite hobby.

"Efficient," he counters, like he thinks that's better.

I roll my eyes but grab my notebook anyway. Our routine has become easy, almost domestic, which is terrifying. I shouldn't be this comfortable around him. He's leaving; I know he's leaving. But comfort has its own gravity, like a planet pulling you into orbit before you realize you're falling.

By noon, the storm softens to drizzle, like it's running out of things to say. We climb to the roof together, trading tools and insults in equal measure. The wind tastes like salt and stubbornness, like the ocean is having an argument with the sky.

He moves like the structure trusts him; I follow carefully, pretending I don't glance at his hands more than I should, pretending I'm not memorizing the way his forearms flex when he hammers, pretending my heart isn't doing some kind of interpretive dance behind my ribs.

"You're not afraid of heights?" he asks, like he's just noticed I'm up here with him.

"Of falling, maybe," I admit. "Of trusting someone else to catch me—definitely."

He pauses, hammer mid-air. For a moment, only the rain speaks between us, and then he says, quietly, "You shouldn't need anyone to catch you."

"Maybe not," I answer, nailing down a shingle like I'm trying to prove a point, "but it's nice when someone tries."

His silence lasts long enough that I think he's retreating again, back behind those walls he's so good at building, but then he says, "You shouldn't have to try alone."

I glance at him, but he's already turned back to work, like admitting that cost him something he couldn't afford to spend.

By dusk, the leak is sealed and the sky is apologizing with streaks of gold and pink, like it's sorry for being so dramatic earlier. We sit on the roof edge, feet dangling, sharing Nonna's leftover frittata and one bottle of lemonade that's mostly water but feels fancy anyway.

The ocean below looks calmer than either of us deserves, rolling gently like it's learned something about patience.

"Do you ever stop?" I ask, watching the waves.

He takes another sip of lemonade like he's buying time. "Stopping feels dangerous."

"Why?"

"Stillness lets the noise in," he says, and I know he's not talking about the storm.

I look out at the horizon, thinking of all the noise I've outrun—expectations, deadlines, heartbreaks wrapped in polite emails that somehow hurt more than angry ones. "Sometimes it's the only way to hear the good parts," I say softly.

He doesn't answer, but his hand brushes mine as he passes the bottle back. It's accidental on purpose, and my pulse forgets how to behave, forgets its job, forgets everything except the warmth of his skin against mine.

When the first star appears, I make a wish I don't admit even to my playlist, something about roofs and rain and hands that brush when they shouldn't.

Then I climb down, heart lighter and heavier at once, like I've found something I wasn't looking for and now I'm not sure what to do with it.

Today's Playlist:

"Polite Rain" – Storm Acoustics in Minor Key

"Caffeine Diplomacy" – Morning Brew Blues

"Accidental on Purpose" – Hand Brush Harmony

Day 25 — West

There's a rhythm to renovation: break, build, breathe, repeat. But lately, the beat skips when Luna laughs. I blame Moose. He's the one who insists on sitting beside her while she paints, tail sweeping in approval every time she hums something that sounds suspiciously like optimism. I try to focus on the wiring in Room Four, but her voice threads through the air like a song I can't tune out, like it's rewiring my brain while I'm literally rewiring the building.

She's wearing one of my spare flannels over her sundress—claims it's for warmth, but it looks like a promise I didn't mean to make, like she's wearing a piece of me without realizing how much that means.

"Wire's live," I warn as she edges closer with that paintbrush like it's a weapon of mass destruction and emotional chaos.

"I trust you," she says, like it's the most natural thing in the world, like she doesn't know that trust is heavier than any tool I carry.

"Bad policy," I say, because someone has to be the voice of reason around here.

"Better than no policy," she counters, and I can't argue with that logic.

The wire behaves. My heartbeat doesn't.

By afternoon, the inn smells like paint and progress and something else that feels dangerously like hope. Luna's playlists have migrated into my head; I catch myself humming something called "Patience and Power Tools" while measuring trim. I pretend I don't notice. Moose notices, the traitor, and gives me a look that says "I knew it."

Nonna brings lemonade and wisdom like she's running some kind of underground operation of emotional sabotage and refreshments. "You both work like people who have something to prove," she says, studying us like we're specimens in her laboratory of human behavior. "Good. Prove it to yourselves first."

37

Then she disappears, leaving us blushing like teenagers who got caught holding hands, which we weren't. Not yet, anyway.

We break for lunch on the porch. The rain has gone, replaced by a shy sun that peeks through the clouds like it's not sure it's supposed to be here. Luna leans back against the railing, eyes closed, face tilted up like she's trying to catch sunlight on her skin.

I can't look away. I should look away. I don't.

"You ever think about after?" she asks suddenly, and the question hangs in the air between us like smoke.

"After what?"

"The thirty days," she says, opening her eyes, and they're too bright, too hopeful, too much for me to handle right now. "What happens when it's done?"

I should say something neutral, safe. "You'll open the inn. I'll move on to the next job." The words are right there, practiced and easy.

She nods like she expected it, but something in her face falls like a bird shot from the sky. "Right. Simple."

But the word simple sounds like a lie between us, sounds like something we're both pretending to believe because the truth is too complicated, too scary, too real.

Later, Moose and I run out for supplies. I tell myself the distance will clear my head, but it just gives the silence room to talk, room to remind me of Seattle and the life I thought I wanted before this place, before her.

Seattle calls again. The phone buzzes in my pocket like a reminder of a different life, a different me. I almost answer this time, almost reach for the escape hatch I've been keeping handy.

I don't.

Back at the inn, Luna's asleep on the couch, one hand tangled in Moose's fur like she's anchoring herself to something real. Her playlists hum softly from the speaker—something slow, hopeful, unguarded. The kind of music that makes you want to believe in happy endings.

I stand there longer than I should, watching her chest rise and fall, and feel something repair itself in me without permission, something I didn't know was broken until it started to heal.

I leave her a note on the workbench: "Roof secure. You did good today." I sign it with a doodle of Moose's paw print because that feels safer than my name, safer than admitting how much I'm starting to care.

When I get home, I pour whiskey and stare at the ceiling, like it has answers. Thirty days is supposed to mean distance. Instead, it feels like countdown to collision, like we're two trains on the same track and neither of us is willing to switch tracks.

Moose sighs in his sleep like he understands everything and isn't worried at all. The ocean answers with its steady rhythm, like it's seen this story before and knows how it ends.

Tomorrow, I promise the ceiling, I'll keep my distance. I'll be professional. I'll remember that I have a life waiting for me somewhere else.

The ceiling doesn't believe me. To be honest, neither do I.

Today's Playlist:
"Rhythm and Renovation" – Construction Heartbeat
"Promise Flannel" – Emotional Wardrobe Malfunction
"Countdown to Collision" – Two Trains, One Track

Day 24 — Luna

The inn smells like new beginnings—and wet dog. "Moose, that was clean tile five seconds ago," I sigh, watching his pawprints march across the lobby like he's leaving a trail of breadcrumbs for his own adventures. He looks smug about it, tail wagging like he just committed the perfect crime.

West, naturally, does not notice; he's elbow-deep in a toolbox that looks like it's plotting world domination and possibly a hostile takeover of the entire hardware store.

"You said you wanted authenticity," West says without looking up, like he has eyes in the back of his head and possibly superpowers.

"I wanted charm, not chaos," I shoot back.

He grunts. "Same thing."

Somewhere in the kitchen, Nonna's radio plays a dramatic Italian ballad about doomed love and perfectly cooked risotto, because of course she does. I hum along, mostly to annoy West, and partially because the song is ridiculously catchy.

He finally glances at me, that half-smile hovering like an eclipse he refuses to admit exists. "What?"

"You don't like a soundtrack?" I ask, innocent as a puppy who just chewed your favorite shoes.

"I prefer silence."

"Silence is for crime scenes and bad dates," I say, dipping my brush into primer, leaving streaks like white hope on the wall. "And this is neither."

He smirks—barely, but it's there, like he's letting a crack of light through his fortress of sarcasm. Progress.

By midmorning, we're in a comfortable rhythm: me narrating the project like a low-budget HGTV host who's had too much coffee, him pretending he's not listening but definitely listening because he keeps correcting my measurements under his breath.

40

I'm explaining the concept of coastal modern with emotional damage when Kelsey bursts in with a tray of coffees and the energy of a caffeinated hurricane who just discovered she has unlimited refills.

"Emergency delivery," she declares. "Also, there's gossip."

"Does it involve Moose?" I ask, because these days, most things do.

"Everything involves Moose. He's basically local royalty now. Brenda from the bakery is making him custom dog biscuits shaped like little bones but with Italian flags on them. Don't ask."

She hands West a cup labeled "Brooding Blend." He reads it, deadpan. "Cute."

"Yours says 'Optimism Overdose,'" Kelsey tells me.

"Accurate." I take a sip and grin. "Tastes like delusion and cinnamon."

When she leaves, the building feels quieter but not empty. West checks the trim along the windows, his sleeves rolled up, revealing forearms that could have their own fan club and probably already do. I keep painting and try not to notice that I've created a playlist called "Distraction Tactics" and "Reasons I Shouldn't Stare at His Forearms."

By afternoon, the wall is done and my patience is not. I set my brush down and stretch, nearly colliding with West as he steps back from the ladder like we're in some kind of romantic comedy blooper reel.

"Careful," he says, steadying the paint can before it tips, his hand brushing mine.

"Careful is my middle name," I say, trying to ignore the electricity that zings up my arm like I've stuck a fork in an outlet.

He raises an eyebrow. "Really?"

"No. It's Francesca. But 'Careful' sounds less like I was named after a soap opera heroine who probably had way more drama than I do."

The corner of his mouth twitches. "Could've been worse."

"Yeah," I say. "Could've been Ethel."

That earns a quiet laugh—the kind that sneaks up and feels like a win, like I've just unlocked an achievement in "Making West Harding Almost Smile."

When the sun dips, we clean up together in companionable silence. Moose guards the door like the unpaid intern he is, occasionally sighing dramatically like we're not working fast enough to suit his schedule.

West loads tools into his truck while I label the last paint can. The label reads "Day 24 — Mostly Functional, Accidentally Flirtatious."

Before I finish, I add in parentheses: "(Love It or List It: Emotional Edition)."

He spots it, and I swear I see the ghost of a smile playing around his mouth. "Accurate."

"See?" I grin. "Honesty is the foundation of every great renovation. And possibly every terrible romance."

He shakes his head, but I catch the smile as he climbs into the truck, not quite hiding it fast enough. "Tomorrow?" he asks.

"Tomorrow," I echo, already plotting a playlist called "Emotional Scaffolding" and wondering if he's secretly looking forward to it as much as I am.

Today's Playlist:
"Wet Dog Authenticity" – Chaos in C Major
"Brooding Blend" – Dark Roast Grumpiness
"Emotional Scaffolding" – Under Construction Love

Day 23 — West

The morning starts with the sound of Moose snoring and the smell of burnt toast—mine, because I was stupid enough to trust a rental toaster that looks like it survived the Cold War and possibly the actual Cold War. I scrape off the evidence, pour coffee strong enough to dissolve guilt and maybe small metal objects, and head to the inn like a man marching to his own execution.

Luna's already there, barefoot on a drop cloth, hair up in a messy bun that's clearly one paint smudge away from modern art. She's balancing a paint tray and singing into a roller handle like it's a microphone, like she's performing at Madison Square Garden instead of in a dusty room that smells like primer and questionable decisions.

Moose, of course, joins in with a howl that sounds suspiciously like backup vocals.

"Backup vocals," I say, leaning against the doorframe like I'm trying to be casual and failing spectacularly.

She jumps, spilling a bit of paint like she's guilty of something. "Don't sneak up like that."

"I knocked."

"You glared," she says, like glaring is somehow the same as knocking.

"Same thing," I deadpan, because arguing with her is becoming my favorite form of self-torture.

I take a sip of coffee and nod at the wall she's painting. "You missed a spot."

She points the roller at me like it's a weapon of mass destruction and social embarrassment. "Careful, or I'll give you a polka-dot shirt."

"Please don't. This is my good pessimism shirt."

She snorts. "You have a shirt for that?"

"I have a shirt for everything. Even for people who rename paint colors 'Brighter Than My Doubts.'"

43

She grins, and it's like the sun came out from behind the clouds specifically to annoy me. "It's called branding."

"Of course it is," I say, but I'm smiling and I hate myself for it.

The banter feels easy, practiced, like we've been doing this for years instead of days. I shouldn't like it. I do. I like it way too much.

We fall into our usual rhythm—her playlist humming under her breath, me trying not to look at her too long, failing miserably. She hums a pop song I don't know but find myself nodding along to anyway.

I mutter something about music being too cheerful before nine a.m., like I'm actually eighty years old and disapprove of everything.

"Let me guess," she says, swiping paint with the confidence of someone who's never met a color she couldn't conquer. "You listen to podcasts about unsolved murders and unseasoned coffee."

"Close. Structural engineering and unseasoned coffee," I correct, like that's somehow better.

"Tragic," she says, like I just confessed to wearing socks with sandals.

The day unfolds in sawdust and sarcasm, which I'm beginning to think is my love language, not that I'll ever admit that out loud. Nonna swings by around noon with sandwiches and scandal from the neighbor's cat situation, then leaves us alone with our projects and a fresh layer of awkward possibility that feels like it might catch fire if we're not careful.

Around two, Luna climbs a ladder to tape the ceiling line, reaching like she's trying to touch the sky or at least the very top of the room.

"If I fall," she calls down, "tell my playlists I loved them. Also, tell Moose he can have my collection of paint swatches."

"Noted," I say, trying to sound professional and not at all concerned. "But Moose gets custody."

"Of the playlists or the emotional baggage?" she asks, and I laugh before I can stop myself.

"Same thing," I answer.

She laughs so hard she nearly drops the tape, swaying on the ladder like she's drunk on optimism and paint fumes. I steady the ladder without thinking, my hand brushing her ankle, and we both freeze for a second like we've been shocked.

Later, we take a break on the porch. She hands me iced coffee in a mason jar labeled "Pessimism with a Chance of Hope." I don't ask where she finds the time for this nonsense, but I drink it anyway because it's good and because she made it.

"This is decent," I admit, which for me is practically a marriage proposal.

"High praise," she says. "From a man who ranks toast as a food group."

"Toast is a lifestyle," I correct, dead serious.

When she laughs, it's the sound of a building remembering what sunlight feels like, the sound of something coming back to life.

We finish the day patching trim and avoiding eye contact that lasts too long. At five, she packs up the brushes with the precision of someone who's organized her entire life into color-coded systems. I log tool inventory, pretending the order matters more than the quiet between us, pretending I'm not counting the minutes until I have to leave but not wanting to.

Moose sprawls across the floor, paws twitching, dreaming of prosciutto and chaos and possibly world domination.

"Tomorrow?" she asks, and it sounds like both a question and a hope.

"Tomorrow," I say, and it feels like a promise I'm not sure I can keep but want to anyway.

On the drive home, I play a jazz station by mistake. I let it play anyway, because it reminds me of her, of the way she moves, of the way she's changing everything I thought I knew about what I wanted.

Today's Playlist:
"Burnt Toast Regrets" – Breakfast Blues

"Roller Handle Microphone" – Construction Karaoke
"Pessimism with Hope" – Iced Coffee Confessions

Day 22 — Luna

Today the inn smells like possibility and paint thinner—an intoxicating combination if you ignore the mild headache that's definitely from the fumes and not from emotional turmoil. I open the front door to let the sea breeze barter with the chemical warfare happening indoors, humming along to my latest playlist, "Hope, but Make It Rollers."

West walks in mid-twirl, like he's just caught me doing something shameful, which honestly, dancing with a paint roller probably counts as.

"You're going to pass out before noon," he says, with the kind of concern that sounds like criticism.

"I prefer to think of it as achieving creative euphoria," I counter, doing another twirl for good measure because I'm nothing if not committed to the bit.

He snorts. "From paint fumes?"

"From progress," I say, pointing the roller at him like it's Excalibur and I'm about to knight him Sir Grumpy of Construction. "Also, possibly from the mini-muffins I ate for breakfast. They were mostly sugar and existential crisis."

I hand him a brush. "We're doing the hallway. Pick a side. No brooding allowed before coffee."

He lifts his coffee cup like it's a shield. "Too late."

Nonna appears like a fairy godmother who believes in hydration and unsolicited advice, probably because she's Italian and believes both are sacred duties. She's carrying smoothies that look like pond water but probably contain enough vegetables to make a rabbit feel virtuous.

"Eat something green," she orders, setting down two glasses that look like they're judging my life choices.

"Is this spinach?" I ask, poking mine suspiciously.

47

"And kale," she says proudly, like she's just discovered the fountain of youth and it's green.

West eyes his smoothie like it might attack him. "Did it offend you first?"

"You'll live longer," she replies, patting his shoulder like he's a fragile child who needs encouragement.

"I'm not sure that's the goal," he mutters, but he drinks it anyway. I swear his jaw tightens in protest, like he's mentally calculating the structural integrity of his dignity versus the nutritional value of kale.

I sip mine, pretend it's fine, then whisper to Moose, "If I start photosynthesizing, water me twice a day and don't let Nonna put me in a salad."

The morning unfolds in brush strokes and banter, the kind of easy rhythm that feels like we've been doing this forever. West fixes a warped doorframe with the concentration of a surgeon defusing a bomb; I attempt to convince the lobby to sparkle through sheer optimism and the magic of good lighting.

Every so often he hums a line from the radio without realizing it, and I count those hums like proof that the world can still surprise you, like evidence that he's softening under all that practical armor.

"Why do you name all your playlists?" he asks around noon, while we're taking a break that involves more staring at each other than actually resting.

"It's how I catalog my emotions," I say. "Therapy, but cheaper and with better background music."

"Does it work?" he asks, and there's genuine curiosity in his voice.

"Cheaper or therapy?"

He almost smiles, and it's like watching the sun come out from behind clouds that have been hanging around forever. "Both."

"Most days," I shrug. "Some days, it's just noise with better marketing."

After lunch, Kelsey drops by with paint chips and chaos, which is basically her brand. "Town council approved your signage permit," she announces, pulling out paperwork like she's a magician pulling rabbits out of hats. "And Brenda from the bakery says she'll cater the opening if you promise not to paint over the ivy."

"The ivy's history," I tell her, examining a paint chip that's definitely too beige for my emotional needs.

"So is Brenda's ex, but she still talks about him," Kelsey quips, grabbing a paint chip that's alarmingly neon. "This one. It says 'I'm fun but I'm also having a quarter-life crisis.'"

She vanishes before I can respond, leaving behind the scent of coffee and trouble and the distinct feeling that my life has become a community project.

West shakes his head, but there's laughter hiding in the corners of his eyes. "Your friends are exhausting."

"They're also the reason this place is still breathing," I say, and it's true. Without them, I'd be curled in a ball somewhere, crying into a spreadsheet.

We finish late, hands covered in color and humor that feels earned. The hallway glows a shade between sea foam and forgiveness, like we've painted our way into a truce.

I label the leftover can "Day 22 — Kale Smoothies and Unsolicited Hope." Then I smirk and add, "(The HGTV Crossover Episode No One Asked For)."

West reads it and sighs, but it's the kind of sigh that sounds suspiciously like contentment. "You're impossible."

"And yet," I say, grinning because I can't help it, "here you are, not leaving."

He picks up his toolbox, and for a second I think he's going to say something real, something that matters. "Tomorrow, maybe."

"Sure," I reply. "And I'm quitting playlists tomorrow."

We both know we're lying. Moose yawns, spreading dust across the floor like confetti. I drop onto the nearest bench, smiling into the sunset light that paints the room in shades of possibility.

Thirty days sounded like a deadline; now it feels like a song finding its chorus, like we're building something that might actually last.

Tonight's playlist: "Accidental Harmony."

Today's Playlist:

"Creative Euphoria" – Paint Fume Dreams

"Kale Smoothie Courage" – Green Machine Guilt

"Accidental Harmony" – Hallway Serenade

Just as West is about to leave, the inn's front door jingles. Nonna's rule: if you're working, you answer the door. If you're not working, you still answer the door because small towns don't believe in boundaries.

"I'll get it," I say, setting down my paintbrush.

When I walk into the lobby, I freeze. Standing there, looking exactly the same except for about three more grey hairs and a wedding ring, is Chloe Reynolds. My best friend from high school. The one who stayed when I left.

"Luna?" Her eyes go wide. "Oh my god, you're back!"

"Chloe! What are you doing here?"

"Nonna called me," she says, pulling me into a hug that smells like lavender and the bakery she runs downtown. "Said something about needing moral support and also that my favorite traitor was back in town."

"I prefer 'prodigal daughter.'"

"Traitor sounds more dramatic." Chloe steps back, looking me over. "Wow. You look... city. Is that an actual designer coat?"

"Don't judge the coat. It was expensive and makes me feel sophisticated."

"Sophisticated doesn't work in Harbor Street," she says with a grin. "Here, sophisticated just means you know how to properly season chowder."

West appears in the doorway of the room we're painting, tool belt slung low on his hips, looking like every small town romance hero cliché come to life. "Everything okay out here?"

"Chloe, this is West. West, this is Chloe, my high school best friend and current town gossip."

"Only current?" Chloe raises an eyebrow. "I'll have to work on that." She extends a hand to West. "Nice to meet you. I've heard a lot about you."

"All good, I hope," West says, but there's tension in his shoulders that wasn't there a minute ago.

"Mostly," Chloe says, her eyes dancing with mischief. "Luna had quite the crush on you in high school."

"Chloe!" My face is on fire. "You promised you'd never talk about that!"

"Technically I promised not to talk about it in high school," she says cheerfully. "Statute of limitations has definitely expired."

West is trying hard not to smile and failing spectacularly. "Is that so?"

"No," I say firmly. "It is not so. Chloe is delusional and also terrible at keeping secrets."

"Hey! I kept plenty of secrets," Chloe says, then her expression softens. "Including why you really left."

The air goes thick with all the things we don't talk about. Boston. Kevin. The job that fell through. The life that was supposed to work but didn't.

"So, the bakery," I say, changing the subject so fast I almost give myself whiplash. "How is it? Still making those croissants that should be illegal?"

"Now we're talking illegal croissants," Chloe says, grateful for the change of topic. "Business is good. Got a new espresso machine that makes West jealous."

"It's not jealousy," West calls from the painting room. "It's professional appreciation for quality equipment."

"Right," Chloe says to me in a stage whisper. "He comes in every morning and pretends he's just 'checking on the building's structural integrity' but really he's there for the cappuccinos."

"Listen," Chloe says, her tone turning serious again. "Nonna's having her annual Fall Festival planning meeting tomorrow night at the bakery. You should come."

"I don't know..."

"Oh, come on. It'll be like old times. Brenda from the post office will be there, Mayor Thompson, everyone. We can catch up properly." She lowers her voice. "Besides, I think Nonna's planning something."

"With Nonna, she's always planning something."

"True, but this time I think you're the target."

After Chloe leaves with a promise to bring croissants tomorrow, I go back to the painting room where West is cleaning brushes.

"You know," he says without looking at me, "you never told me you had a crush on me in high school."

I almost drop the paint roller. "That was a long time ago."

"Still." He finally looks at me, and there's something in his eyes I can't quite read. "I wish you'd told me back then."

The air between us shifts, thick with all the unspoken words and missed opportunities. For a minute, I think he might say something else, might close the distance between us.

Then my phone buzzes - it's Nonna with a text that just says, "Fall Festival. Tomorrow. Be there or I'll tell West about your diary from 10th grade."

I show the text to West, and he laughs. "Your grandmother plays dirty."

"She learned from the best."

But something has shifted between us, something important. The walls are coming down, literally and figuratively.

Today's Playlist:
"Secret Crush Confessions" – High School Flashbacks
"Text Message Blackmail" – Nonna's Threats
"Walls Coming Down" – Literally and Figuratively

Day 21 — West

The thing about old buildings is they don't lie—they just groan the truth until you finally listen. Today, the truth is that the wiring in Room Six was designed by someone who believed in chaos as an art form, probably after drinking way too much coffee and deciding electricity was more of a suggestion than a science.

Luna peeks around the door, holding a tray of muffins like she's some kind of construction angel who descended from heaven to save me from myself and this wiring nightmare.

"I brought peace offerings," she says, like I'm a wild animal she's trying to tame.

I gesture to the tangle of wires that looks like a metal octopus had a nervous breakdown. "Unless those muffins are also electricians, we're beyond peace. We're in full-on warfare territory."

She steps closer, unbothered by the chaos that's currently making my eye twitch. "Chocolate chip diplomacy works in ninety percent of conflicts."

"And the other ten?"

"Explosions," she grins, like explosions are a perfectly acceptable outcome. "You want one?"

"An explosion or a muffin?"

"Yes," she says, because of course she does.

I take the muffin. It's still warm, and the scent does things to my self-control I'm not proud of. It's like my brain and my stomach are having a heated argument about priorities.

"Not bad," I admit, which for me is basically saying "this is the best thing I've ever eaten and I would die for it."

"High praise from the man who thinks toast is haute cuisine," she says, and I can hear the smile in her voice.

"Toast never betrays you," I say, like I'm defending toast's honor.

"Clearly you've never burned one," she counters.

I give her a look. "You'd be surprised."

She sits on the window ledge, watching me work, sipping coffee that smells like optimism and regret and probably other emotions I'm not ready to examine. "You ever do anything that isn't fixing things?"

"Not if I can help it," I say, because it's the truth. Fixing things is easier than fixing myself.

"That's sad," she says, and it's so direct, so unexpected, that it actually hurts a little.

"That's practical," I counter, because practical is safer than sad.

She tilts her head, studying me like I'm a complex equation she's determined to solve. "You know, for a man allergic to joy, you have decent taste in muffins."

"I'm evolving," I say, and I'm not entirely joking.

Moose sneezes from the hallway, punctuating the moment like he's adding his own commentary to our conversation.

She laughs, and I almost drop a wire nut because the sound hits me somewhere in the chest I didn't know was vulnerable. "That was Moose's contribution to the discussion."

By noon, we've got the circuits behaving and the room smelling less like despair and more like accomplishment. Luna starts scraping old paint from the window frame, humming something that sounds suspiciously like a love song, and I'm trying to focus on junction boxes but I keep getting distracted by the way she bites her lip when she's concentrating.

"Stop humming," I say, trying to sound annoyed and failing.

"You'll distract the wiring," she adds, like she's actually concerned about the emotional state of electrical systems.

"Are you blaming the electrical system for your focus issues?" I ask, and I'm actually smiling now.

"Healthy," she smirks, and I lose all ability to form coherent sentences for a solid ten seconds.

Around two, Nonna appears with lemonade and unsolicited moral commentary, because apparently that's her role in this domestic drama we've accidentally created. "You both look tired," she says, like we're children who need a nap. "Maybe you should talk about your feelings instead of pretending to fix things."

Luna nearly drops her scraper. "Nonna!"

"What? I am old. I have no time for denial," she says, patting my shoulder like she's blessing me or possibly cursing me, it's hard to tell with Italian grandmothers.

I cough into my hand, trying to hide the fact that she just called me out so accurately it's almost impressive. "We're fine. It's just a circuit."

She eyes me like she can smell deflection the way sharks smell blood in the water. "Yes. A circuit of emotion. Breakers tripped."

Then she's gone, muttering about mortals and muffins and the emotional incompetence of people under the age of seventy.

When the door closes, Luna groans. "She's worse than therapy."

"She's cheaper than therapy," I point out, which is probably not the right thing to say but is definitely true.

"Barely," Luna says, but she's smiling.

We work through the afternoon, the silence between us a mix of concentration and whatever this slow burn thing is we're pretending not to notice. Every time she laughs or hums or says something ridiculous about playlists, I feel another crack in the wall I've spent years building around myself.

Around five, she labels the new paint sample jar "Day 21 — Shockingly Functional."

"Appropriate," I say, because somehow she always manages to nail it.

"You like it?" she asks, and there's hope in her voice that makes something in my chest tighten.

"I like that you're consistent," I say, which is true and also the safest compliment I can offer.

Her smile softens, like she understands what I'm not saying. "Consistency is my love language."

"I thought it was playlists," I say, and I'm definitely smiling now.

"That too," she says, and we stand there for a moment, the air thick with things we're not saying.

We clean up in silence. Moose noses at the muffin crumbs like he's auditing them for quality control purposes. When Luna locks up for the day, I find myself walking slower toward the truck, trying to stretch out this moment, this day.

"Tomorrow?" she asks, and it sounds like a question and a prayer.

"Tomorrow," I say. "Bring fewer muffins."

"Never," she says, and her laugh follows me down the steps, light enough to make the air feel less heavy, like she's somehow making the world brighter just by being in it.

At home, I don't even turn on the murder podcast. I just sit there with Moose, listening to the hum of the ocean and the sound of something inside me rewiring itself, something I didn't even know was broken until she started fixing it.

Today's Playlist:
"Wiring Warfare" – Electrical Chaos Blues
"Chocolate Chip Diplomacy" – Muffin Negotiations
"Evolving" – Surprisingly Not Hating Everything

Day 20 — Luna

The storm passes overnight, leaving the inn smelling like wet wood and second chances. I wake to the sound of hammers—West, of course, refusing to let the building sleep in like it's a lazy teenager who needs to learn responsibility.

I shuffle into the lobby with coffee strong enough to baptize mistakes and possibly exorcise ghosts. He's already balanced on a ladder, sleeves rolled, forearms glinting with sawdust and judgment, looking entirely too attractive for this early in the morning.

"Morning," I call. "Did the storm sign off on this noise permit?"

"Daylight's burning," he says, like he's personally offended by the concept of rest. "We lost twelve hours yesterday."

I sip, wince, and grin. "Some people lose socks. You lose half a day and start a crusade."

"Deadlines don't care about sentiment," he says, like deadlines are his religion.

"Neither does espresso," I counter, "but I still drink it. We all have our vices."

He smirks, a rare, reluctant sunrise that makes my stomach do something complicated. "You're impossible before caffeine."

"I'm impossible after caffeine too," I say. "I'm consistently impossible. It's part of my brand."

We fall into rhythm—him patching the ceiling, me sanding trim. Outside, the gulls sound like they're auditioning for chaos, like they're providing the soundtrack to our renovation drama. Inside, the air hums with paint dust and proximity and the kind of tension that's either going to lead to amazing things or a complete emotional breakdown.

Nonna enters carrying a clipboard like a general preparing for battle. "We need a plan," she declares, like we haven't been planning for twenty days straight. "Supplies, invoices, and a miracle. Probably multiple miracles."

"We're fresh out of miracles," West says, deadpan.

"Then find discounts," she says, marching out again, leaving behind the faint smell of lavender and intimidation.

West glances at me, and I swear he looks genuinely terrified. "She terrifies me."

"Good," I say, grinning because I live for these moments. "Means she likes you. Nonna only intimidates people she thinks are worth her time."

He climbs down, wipes his hands, and studies the wall like it holds the secrets of the universe. "We're short on the roof decking order. If it doesn't arrive by Wednesday, the whole schedule collapses."

"Can we borrow from another supplier?" I ask, already mentally calculating alternative plans.

"I'll try," he says, rubbing his jaw like he's physically trying to relieve the stress. "But this might cut into your 'make it pretty' phase."

I look at the ceiling, the scars of old leaks and new patches that tell a story of survival. "Pretty is overrated. I'll settle for standing."

He glances down, and his eyes are soft for a second, like he sees more than just the building, like he sees me. "That's what you said about Boston, isn't it?"

The words land softer than they should, like he knows more than he should, like he's been paying attention to the things I don't say out loud.

"Standing isn't the same as living," I say, and it's the most honest thing I've said all week.

He nods slowly, like he's filing that away with every other quiet truth he's not ready to say out loud. When the deck supplier calls back with a week's delay, we sit on the porch steps, eating Nonna's emergency biscotti and pretending it's not a problem.

"So," I say, trying to sound optimistic and probably failing. "What's Plan B?"

"Work around it. Focus on the wiring. The railing inspection's due Friday."

"And Plan C?"

"Pray," he says, like it's a legitimate construction strategy.

"Nonna's got that covered," I say. "She's probably already lighting candles and blessing the power tools."

He half-smiles, and it's like watching ice melt in springtime. "You're not worried?"

"I'm too stubborn for worry," I say, because it's true. Worrying doesn't fix anything, but stubbornness definitely does.

He studies me for a long beat, like he's trying to figure out how I work, like I'm some kind of complex machine he needs to understand before he can fix. "That might be your problem."

"Or my secret weapon," I counter.

Moose barks once, like he's voting for optimism. West mutters, "Traitor," and I hide a grin behind my mug like a teenager with a crush.

By sunset, the building hums again, alive with possibility and the scent of progress. I write in my notebook: Day 20—short on materials, long on faith. And maybe, just maybe, long on something else that's starting to feel like hope.

Today's Playlist:

"Crusade Against Rest" – Hammer Time Anxiety

"Consistently Impossible" – Branding My Chaos

"Reroute and Rise" – Optimism in D Minor

Day 19 — West

Inspections. My least favorite part of any project, mostly because they remind me of Seattle and everything I'm trying to outrun. The inspector, Tom, shows up with a clipboard, a smirk, and what appears to be a personal vendetta against efficiency and my general happiness.

He runs his meter over every outlet like he's searching for moral failure in the wiring, like he's trying to catch the building in a lie. "GFCIs?" he asks, like he already knows the answer and is just enjoying the power.

"Ordered. On backorder," I say, trying to sound professional and not like I want to throw his clipboard out the window.

"Handrails?"

"Coming tomorrow."

"Exit signage?"

"Already installed."

He makes a note on his clipboard with a pen that looks suspiciously like a weapon. "You're cutting it close, Harding."

"Story of my life," I say, because it's true and because I'm too tired to pretend otherwise.

Luna appears mid-checklist with two mugs and a smile that could sell forgiveness by the gallon and possibly world peace. "Coffee break?" she asks, like she's an angel of mercy sent to rescue me from bureaucratic hell.

Tom beams like she just offered him a promotion. "Don't mind if I do."

I glare at the betrayal happening in real time, like my own personal construction assistant has just defected to the enemy. "We're mid-inspection."

"People work better caffeinated," she says, like this is a scientific fact she's researched extensively.

61

"Some people work better quiet," I counter, but she's already handing me a mug that smells like hope and rebellion.

"You're not 'some people,'" she says, and she's right, which is annoying.

When Tom finally leaves with a "minor corrections" note that feels like a judgment on my entire existence, I groan and consider moving to a remote cabin where there are no building codes or inspectors named Tom who clearly hate me.

Luna leans against the doorframe, sipping victory like it's fine wine. "Minor corrections," she mimics. "That's basically an A-plus."

"On what scale?" I ask, genuinely curious about her grading system.

"Mine," she says, like that explains everything.

I shake my head, but there's laughter under it, like she's somehow making this disaster feel like a win. She's chaos. Beautiful, well-intentioned chaos that smells like coffee and optimism.

Moose wanders in, tail wagging like a metronome for my patience, which is currently running on empty. I scratch his head. "At least someone's consistent."

Luna grins. "He just knows where the snacks are."

We return to work with renewed energy, probably fueled by caffeine and the sheer absurdity of the situation. By noon, we've replaced the faulty outlets and adjusted the stair rail. She hums something upbeat that I'm pretending not to like but actually find myself tapping along to. I counter with dry sarcasm until it sounds like we're creating some kind of bizarre harmony.

By sunset, everything's compliant—barely, but compliant enough for Tom and his clipboard of judgment. She writes on the chalkboard by the door: "Day 19—Pass with Personality."

I read it aloud, because I can't help myself. "You're documenting our descent into madness?"

"It's content," she says, like that's a perfectly reasonable explanation.

"Content?"

"Marketing for the opening," she says, like she's already planning the grand reopening that feels both impossible and inevitable.

"Right," I say. "Because the internet needs more of this." I gesture vaguely to the chaos that is our life.

"Exactly," she flashes a grin that could probably power a small city. "Tomorrow: paint or panic?"

"Both," I say, because honesty is important. "In equal measure."

Moose sneezes. Luna laughs. I realize I'm smiling again, a real smile that feels foreign and wonderful all at once. Thirty days left. Maybe less to pretend this isn't becoming something else, something bigger and scarier and more amazing than I ever expected.

Today's Playlist:

"Bureaucratic Hell" – Inspection Anxiety Blues

"Coffee Sabotage" – Caffeinated Betrayal

"Pass with Personality" – Compliance and Chaos

Day 18 — Luna

Dinner on the porch was supposed to be simple—Nonna's lasagna, a borrowed string of lights, and the illusion that we're not both counting down the days like we're waiting for a bomb to either go off or be defused, and at this point I'm not sure which would be better.

I overprepare anyway, because I'm me and I can't do simple like normal people. Matching plates that I've had in storage since college, a table runner that's seen better seasons but has sentimental value, candles that drip faster than my composure, and a playlist called "Risotto & Recklessness" because apparently I'm incapable of not turning everything into a production.

West is already outside when I come out, sleeves rolled, notebook beside his plate like he's planning to audit the meal or possibly grade my lasagna on a scale of one to ten. Moose lies under his chair, sighing dramatically every time we pause between bites, like we're not eating fast enough to suit his royal schedule.

"You cook like you're proving a point," West says, fork hovering over a piece of lasagna like he's analyzing its structural integrity.

"Survival is a point," I sip my lemonade like it's wine and I'm at a fancy restaurant instead of on my grandmother's porch with a man who's systematically dismantling my emotional defenses. "And I'm Italian. Feeding people is my love language. It's genetic. My ancestors communicated through pasta and passive-aggressive compliments."

West laughs, and it's that rare, genuine laugh that makes my stomach do things I'd prefer not to analyze in detail. "That explains Nonna."

"Oh god, Nonna's communication style is like ninety percent food-based emotional manipulation. Remember when she was mad at me about not calling enough? She made me seven different types of biscotti, each one progressively more passive-aggressive."

"What was in the last one?"

64

"Just almond extract and disappointment."

He's still laughing when Moose suddenly sits up, ears perked. A moment later, I hear it too - footsteps on the gravel driveway. Not just any footsteps. The expensive, purposeful kind that spells trouble in designer shoes.

"I thought you said this dinner was just us," I say, already getting a bad feeling.

"It was supposed to be," West says, standing up. "Unless..."

"Unless Nonna decided we needed a chaperone," I finish. "Or a marriage counselor. Or possibly both."

But when the figure steps into the porch light, it's not Nonna. It's Chloe, looking flushed and excited, carrying a bakery box like she's delivering state secrets.

"You're not going to believe this," she says, practically bouncing with energy. "The Fall Festival committee had their emergency meeting tonight."

"Emergency meeting?" West asks. "What was the emergency?"

"Brenda from the post office and Carol from the library are having a feud over who gets to run the kissing booth," Chloe says, setting the box on the table. "It's getting ugly. People are choosing sides."

I stare at her. "A kissing booth feud? In 2024?"

"This is Harbor Street," Chloe says patiently. "We move at our own pace. Also, the town council voted that you and West should be in charge of resolving the conflict."

"What?" West and I say at the same time.

"Apparently they think you two have... experience with tension resolution," Chloe says, trying and failing to keep a straight face. "Brenda specifically mentioned that you two look at each other like you're either about to kiss or kill each other, and she's not sure which but she'd like to find out."

I want the ground to swallow me whole. "Brenda needs to mind her business."

"She says the whole town's business is her business," Chloe says helpfully. "Also, she made cookies for the meeting. They're very persuasive."

"This is ridiculous," West says, but he's smiling. "We're not running a kissing booth mediation service."

"That's what I told them," Chloe says, opening the bakery box. "But then Mayor Thompson pointed out that the festival raises money for the town library, and Carol from the library started crying about how the children need books, and honestly, it was emotionally manipulative and effective."

She slides a plate of cookies toward us. "So, what's the verdict? Are you going to save the festival and possibly get Brenda and Carol to make up, or are you going to let the children suffer without new books?"

I look at West, who's trying hard not to laugh and mostly succeeding. The problem is, I'm not sure if he's laughing at the situation or at my complete and utter humiliation.

"We'll think about it," I say finally.

Chloe beams. "Great! I'll tell them you're considering it. Meanwhile, I brought peace offerings." She gestures toward the cookies. "These are the 'please mediate our town drama' cookies. They have extra chocolate chips."

After Chloe leaves, West picks up a cookie. "You know, in Boston, this would probably be considered harassment."

"In Harbor Street, it's community involvement," I say, taking a cookie myself. "Also, these are really good cookies."

"They are," he agrees. "But we're not running a kissing booth mediation service."

"Definitely not."

We sit in silence for a minute, eating cookies and pretending we're not thinking about what Chloe said. About how the whole town sees this tension between us. About Brenda's observation that we look at each other like we're about to kiss or kill each other.

"So," West says finally, "hypothetically, if we were to help with this festival disaster..."

"Hypothetically," I confirm.

"What would that even look like?"

I think about it. "Probably involves sitting in a room with two elderly women who are having a turf war over a charity kissing booth. Probably involves a lot of passive-aggressive compliments. Probably involves Nonna showing up with more food-based emotional manipulation."

West smiles. "Sounds like a typical Tuesday."

The thing is, as ridiculous as this situation is, there's something comforting about it. In Boston, my problems were career deadlines and relationship drama and trying to figure out who I was supposed to be. Here, my problems are kissing booth feuds and biscotti-based emotional manipulation and the fact that the man sitting across from me makes my heart do things that should probably be medically concerning.

"You know," I say, "as much as I complain about this town..."

"Yeah?" West looks at me, really looks at me, and I feel that familiar pull, that gravitational force that's been drawing us together since high school.

"It's not so bad," I finish softly. "This place. These people."

"They love you," he says simply. "We've always loved you."

My throat gets tight. "Even when I left?"

"Especially when you left," he says. "Because we knew you'd come back eventually."

And sitting there on the porch, surrounded by string lights and cookie crumbs and the soft sound of waves from the beach, I realize he's right. This isn't just an inn I'm renovating. It's a home I'm returning to.

Today's Playlist: "Kiss Me" by Sixpence None the Richer, "I Melt With You" by Modern English, "There She Goes" by The La's

"Good to know," he says, taking another bite. "Mine's grumbling until the wiring passes inspection."

I laugh. "Very romantic. Nothing says 'I care about you' quite like discussing electrical compliance over dinner."

We eat in comfortable silence, the kind that hums instead of drags. Beyond the porch, the sea keeps breathing, steady and rhythmic like it's been doing this for thousands of years and will continue long after we're gone. The air smells like basil and salt and new beginnings that don't know they're new yet.

I catch myself memorizing his shoulders in the amber light, the way his hair catches the string lights, the lines around his eyes when he almost smiles. I immediately scold my heart for being such a cliché, for falling for the grumpy contractor who's supposed to be temporary, who's supposed to leave in eleven days.

Nonna appears long enough to deliver dessert and a raised eyebrow that says she knows exactly what's happening and she approves, which is both comforting and terrifying. "Stay out of trouble," she says, setting down tiramisu that looks like it was made by angels who have excellent taste in coffee and cocoa. "And remember: love is easier when the roof doesn't leak. But also less interesting."

Then she's gone again, leaving the echo of her advice like the last word in a hymn I'm not sure I believe in but can't stop humming.

West picks up his fork again, but his smile lingers. "She plans these moments, doesn't she?"

"Every emotional ambush is handmade," I say. "She's been matchmaking since before I was born. I think she considers it her spiritual calling."

He chuckles, softer than I've ever heard, and the sound feels like being trusted with a secret, like being given something precious and fragile. When the plates are cleared, we linger, neither of us wanting to break the spell.

West leans back, one boot hooked under the table, his expression somewhere between exhausted and peaceful. The string lights flicker in the breeze, painting his face in warm gold and uncertainty, making him look vulnerable and beautiful and completely dangerous to my emotional stability.

"So," I say, because the silence is getting too thick, too full of things we're not saying. "Tell me something true."

He hesitates, like truth is a currency he doesn't spend often. "You first."

"Okay." I think for a moment, searching for something real, something that matters. "I miss Boston sometimes, but not the version of me that lived there. Does that count?"

He studies me, like he's measuring the weight of my words. "You can do better than that."

"Fine," I say, going for something more honest, more vulnerable. "I once broke up with someone because he hated my playlists. He said they were 'chaotic and emotionally excessive.'"

He snorts. "That's fair."

"Your turn," I challenge.

He looks out over the railing, like the answer is written in the waves. "Seattle offered me a promotion. Project manager on a big build."

"Sounds impressive," I say, and it does. It sounds like the kind of life I was supposed to want, the kind of stability I ran away from.

"It is," he says, but he doesn't sound happy about it. "But I'd spend every day designing buildings I'll never see finished. Moving from one temporary project to another."

"You don't like temporary?" I ask, and the question hangs in the air between us, heavy with meaning.

He glances at me, and his eyes are so honest it hurts. "You tell me."

Something in the air thickens—the quiet kind that smells like rain before it happens, like possibility before it becomes reality. I tuck a curl behind my ear and hope the gesture hides how hard my pulse is working, how my heart is trying to beat its way out of my chest.

We hold the moment a heartbeat too long, the space between us charged with everything we're not saying, everything we're afraid to want.

Moose snorts under the table, breaking the spell like the professional emotional sabotage artist he is. We laugh, softer this time, like the sound is afraid to echo too far, like we're both afraid of breaking whatever this is.

When he stands to leave, the porch light flickers and dies, plunging us into darkness that feels intimate and terrifying all at once. I reach for my phone flashlight at the same time he reaches for me.

Our hands brush in the dark. For one impossible second, the air between us feels charged enough to spark, like we're standing in an electrical storm of our own making.

He clears his throat, and his voice is rough. "I'll check the wiring tomorrow."

"Right," I smile, though he can't see it. "Of course you will. Because you're you, and that's what you do."

When he walks away, I whisper to the dark, to the stars, to anyone who's listening, "Tomorrow's going to be trouble."

Today's Playlist:

"Lasagna Auditing" – Structural Pasta Analysis

"Emotional Ambush" – Nonna's Matchmaking

"Half-Light Confessions" – Porch Light Electric

Day 17 — West

The storm held off, but the air feels like it's waiting for something to break. Maybe it's us. Maybe it's the fragile tension that's been building between us for days, the kind that feels like static electricity before lightning strikes.

Luna's already on the roof deck when I get there, barefoot, balancing a paint tray on the railing like she's daring gravity to blink first. She's singing—off-key, of course—but the sound works. It always does. The sunset throws fire across the water, lighting her hair like it's been caught stealing gold from the sky.

"Careful," I call, trying to sound like a responsible contractor and not like a man who's terrified she might fall because he's already falling himself.

"Noted," she glances over her shoulder, grinning. "But you'd try."

She's right. I would. I'd risk everything to catch her, and that realization hits me like a physical blow, like the universe just dropped a truth bomb I'm not ready to handle.

That's when the sky opens up. One minute we're painting in the golden sunset, the next minute we're getting absolutely soaked by a storm that came out of nowhere. Rain comes down in sheets - the kind of relentless coastal rain that feels like the ocean decided to climb into the sky and fall back down all at once.

"Inside!" I shout over the wind, grabbing paint cans and tools while Luna scrambles to collect her supplies. We make it to the stairwell just as lightning cracks across the sky, followed immediately by thunder that shakes the entire building.

We end up in the small storage room on the second floor - the only room that's remotely finished, with boxes piled everywhere and a single bare bulb overhead. It's cramped and dusty and smells like paint and old wood, but it's dry.

"Well," Luna says, wringing out her hair. "That was dramatic."

71

"Coastal weather," I say, trying to catch my breath. "Never predictable."

We're standing too close in the small space, our shoulders almost touching. The storm rages outside, but in here, it's quiet except for the sound of rain on the roof and our breathing, which suddenly seems way too loud.

"You know," Luna says, looking around at the boxes, "this room used to be my mother's sewing room."

I look at her, surprised. "I didn't know that."

"Yeah," she says softly, running her hand over a stack of boxes. "She could make anything. Dresses, curtains, even the wedding dress Nonna still keeps in her closet. She taught me to sew before she..." Luna trails off, and I can see the pain in her eyes, even after all these years.

"I'm sorry," I say, because what else is there to say?

"She was amazing," Luna continues, her voice thick with emotion. "She had this laugh - this big, loud laugh that filled every room she was in. She loved this inn. She used to say that buildings have souls, and that if you listen carefully, you can hear them telling their stories."

The rain continues to fall outside, creating a cocoon around us. In the dim light of the storage room, Luna looks younger, more vulnerable. Like the teenager I knew before she left, before life complicated everything.

"What do you think this building is telling us?" I ask.

Luna smiles, but it's tinged with sadness. "I think it's telling us to come home. Both of us."

She walks over to one of the boxes and carefully opens it. Inside are old photographs, yellowed with age, showing the inn through different decades. Her grandmother as a young woman, her grandfather looking strong and proud, her mother laughing in a garden that's probably long gone.

"Look," she says, pulling out a photo. "This is my parents on their wedding day. Right here on the lawn."

I take the photo. Her parents are young and beautiful and so clearly in love. Her father has his arm around her mother's waist, and they're looking at each other like they're the only two people in the world.

"They were so happy," Luna says quietly.

"They still are," I say gently. "In a different way."

"I know." Luna puts the photo back carefully. "Sometimes I wonder if she'd be proud of me. If she'd understand why I left, why I came back."

"She'd understand," I say, my voice firm. "Because she was brave too. Building a life, running an inn, raising a daughter... that takes courage. Just like coming back here takes courage."

Luna looks at me then, really looks at me, and the space between us feels charged with all the things we haven't said. "Why did you really come back to Harbor Street, West? Don't give me the housing was cheap answer. I want the truth."

I take a deep breath. Because we're here, in this small room with the storm raging outside, surrounded by her family's history, and I think it's time for the truth.

"Because I was hoping you'd come back someday," I say quietly. "Because this town, this place, never felt right without you in it."

Her breath catches. "West..."

"I spent ten years moving from job to job, city to city, trying to find something that felt like home. But everywhere I went, something was missing. And then I realized what it was." I reach out and gently touch her cheek. "It was you."

The storm outside seems to pause, holding its breath. In the storage room, with dust motes dancing in the single light bulb, everything else fades away. There's only us, only this moment, only the truth that's been between us since we were teenagers.

"I've loved you since I was seventeen, Luna," I say, and the words feel like both a confession and a relief. "I loved you when you left, I loved you while you were gone, and I'll love you whether you stay or go."

Tears stream down her face, but she doesn't wipe them away. "You should have told me."

"And what would you have done?" I ask gently. "Would you have stayed? Or would you still have needed to find your own way?"

She doesn't answer, because we both know the answer. She needed to leave, needed to fail, needed to realize that what she was looking for wasn't in Boston after all.

"I'm sorry," she whispers. "For all the years you waited."

"I'd wait forever," I say, and it's the truest thing I've ever said. "But I'm hoping I don't have to."

The storm outside starts to quiet, the rain softening from a downpour to a gentle patter. But in the storage room, another storm is breaking - the one that's been between us for years, full of unspoken words and missed chances and the kind of love that doesn't fade with time or distance.

Luna steps closer, until there's barely any space between us. "I don't want to leave again," she says softly.

"Then don't," I say, and I'm not asking, I'm begging.

"I'm scared," she admits, and her voice is trembling. "What if I'm not strong enough? What if I mess this up? What if I hurt you?"

"What if you don't?" I counter. "What if this is everything we've been waiting for? What if we're exactly where we're supposed to be?"

She looks at me for a long time, her eyes searching mine, looking for answers I hope she finds. Finally, slowly, she leans in and kisses me.

It's not like the other kisses - the tentative ones, the ones full of uncertainty. This kiss is different. It's full of years of wanting, full of all the times we almost said something, full of all the moments that led us here, to this small room during a storm, finally choosing each other.

When we finally pull apart, the rain has stopped completely. Sunlight is breaking through the clouds, casting rainbows across the dusty floor of the storage room.

"Well," Luna says, her voice thick with emotion. "I guess the storm's over."

"Not even close," I say, pulling her back into my arms. "I think it's just beginning.

Today's Playlist: "Storms in Africa" by Toto, "Rainy Days and Mondays" by The Carpenters, "I'll Stand By You" by The Pretenders

We paint in silence for a while, the kind of comfortable quiet that feels earned after weeks of working together, after weeks of learning each other's rhythms and habits and tells. The sea glints below, silver and infinite. Her brushstrokes are wide and sure, like she's been painting her whole life; mine are measured, methodical, like I'm still trying to maintain control in a situation that's rapidly spinning beyond it.

The contrast should irritate me. It doesn't. It feels right, like we're two halves of something that's slowly coming together.

She hums, and I pretend I'm not matching her rhythm, not letting her music seep into my bones, not letting her voice become the soundtrack to my life. I'm failing spectacularly at all of it.

At some point she says, "Do you ever think about what comes after this?" and the question hangs in the air like smoke, like something we both know we should ignore but can't.

"After what?"

"After the thirty days," she says, turning to face me, and her eyes are too bright, too hopeful, too full of everything I'm afraid to want. "What happens when it's done? When the inn is finished? When you leave?"

I should say something neutral, safe. "You'll open the inn. I'll move on to the next job." The words are right there, practiced and easy and completely wrong.

She nods like she expected it, but something in her face falls like a bird with a broken wing. "Right. Simple."

But the word simple sounds like a lie between us, sounds like we're both pretending this is just another job, just another temporary arrangement, when we both know it's so much more than that.

The wind shifts, lifting the edge of her hair like it's trying to touch her, like it knows something we don't. Paint drips onto her wrist; I reach out instinctively, thumb brushing it away before I can stop myself.

Her pulse stumbles under my touch. So does mine.

I try to make a joke about health and safety, about the hazards of painting on roofs, but my voice won't cooperate, won't form the words that would put distance between us again.

"This is a bad idea," I say quietly, and I'm not talking about the paint or the roof or the timing. I'm talking about us, about this feeling that's growing between us like something wild and untamed.

"Definitely," she agrees, but she doesn't move away. She doesn't pull back.

Neither do I.

Then the moment decides for us. The space between us collapses, paint and air and fear forgotten like they never mattered. The kiss starts tentative—curious, unsure, like we're both testing the waters, afraid of drowning—and then deepens with the kind of inevitability you only find once in a lifetime, if you're lucky.

It tastes like salt and surrender, like paint fumes and possibility, like everything I've been running from and everything I've been running toward all at once.

The world tilts; I can't tell if the sea is rising or if I am, if the ground is shifting or if I'm finally finding solid ground after years of drifting.

When we break apart, the sunset's gone, but she's still glowing, her lips parted, her eyes wide like she's just as surprised as I am. I try to steady my breathing; she laughs softly, the sound shaking like a secret, like she can't believe this is happening either.

"You're not so bad at terrible ideas," she says, and her voice is husky, like the kiss stole all the air from her lungs.

"I've had practice," I admit, and it's the truest thing I've said in years.

I want to tell her about Seattle, about the job waiting, about the life I thought I wanted before she showed me what I actually need. But the words stay buried under the weight of this moment, under the feeling of her in my arms, under the knowledge that everything has changed and nothing will ever be the same again.

Moose barks from the stairwell, and we both laugh, the sound shaky but real, like he's reminding us that the world still exists beyond this rooftop, beyond this moment.

"Tomorrow," I tell her, meaning everything and nothing, meaning I don't know what comes next but I want to find out with her.

She nods. "Tomorrow."

For the first time, thirty days feels like both too long and not long enough, like a countdown and a lifeline all at once.

Today's Playlist:

"Gravity Defiance" – Rooftop Rebellion

"Static Electricity" – Pre-Lightning Tension

"Blueprints and Bruises" – Structural Heart Damage

Day 16 — Luna

I wake up before my alarm, which should be illegal on a Saturday or any day that follows a kiss that rewrote the entire operating system of my heart. The first thing I notice is the smell of coffee. The second is that I'm smiling, which feels dangerous and wonderful and completely out of my control.

Last night's kiss keeps replaying on a loop—like one of those movie trailers that refuses to stop autoplaying, except this one is playing in my head and my heart and possibly my soul. I throw on jeans and a paint-splattered hoodie, tell myself the flutter in my chest is caffeine withdrawal, not feelings, but my reflection in the mirror disagrees entirely. My cheeks look like they've been in on the joke since sunrise, like they're broadcasting my emotional state to anyone who cares to look.

Nonna's already in the kitchen when I shuffle in, humming something suspiciously romantic and entirely too knowing. "Sleep well?" she asks without looking up from her mixing bowl, like she hasn't been waiting for this moment my entire life.

"Fine. Normal. Unremarkable," I pour coffee like I'm auditioning for denial, like the burn from the mug can distract from the burn in my chest.

"Good," she says, adding sugar with the precision of someone who's planned this conversation for weeks. "Because I saw West leave the roof at midnight. I assume you were both praying."

I choke on the coffee. "Roof inspection."

"Of course," she smirks, like she knows exactly what kind of inspection was happening. "Your prayers were loud."

Before I can argue, West knocks once and steps in, early, which feels like a statement, like he couldn't stay away even if he tried. His hair is damp from the shower; his shirt is the same one from yesterday,

78

sleeves rolled. Professional. Controlled. Entirely unfair and completely irresistible.

"Morning," he says, nodding like the world didn't tilt on its axis last night, like my entire universe didn't just rearrange itself around the feeling of his lips on mine.

"Morning," I echo, tone two octaves too bright, like I'm trying to convince myself everything is normal. "Coffee?"

He hesitates, then nods. "Sure."

Nonna watches us like a nature documentary narrator who's just discovered a new species of emotionally stunted humans. "Observe the humans attempting composure," she mutters to her mixing bowl. "Fascinating. They think we can't see the unresolved sexual tension from here."

I glare at her. She shrugs, completely unrepentant. "Don't burn the eggs. Or each other."

By the time we get to the lobby, the air between us feels crowded with unsaid things, with memories of last night, with the ghost of his kiss still lingering on my lips. He sets down his toolbox; I clutch my clipboard like it's a shield, like it can protect me from the feelings that are currently staging a coup in my heart.

"So," I say too loudly, like volume can compensate for emotional chaos. "Agenda. Finish the crown molding in Room Two, finalize the trim in the breakfast nook, and pretend last night didn't happen."

He freezes mid-step, and I can see the conflict in his shoulders, in the way his hands tighten on his toolbox. "Pretend what didn't happen?"

"The inspection," I say quickly, like the word isn't completely transparent and pathetic. "You know, the emotional wiring check."

A flicker of amusement breaks through his carefully constructed mask, like sunlight through storm clouds. "Right. That."

We dive into work like it's penance, like we can build walls fast enough to keep our feelings out. He hammers too hard; I paint too fast. Moose, intuitive as ever, sprawls across the hallway like an obstacle course of loyalty and emotional support, occasionally sighing like he's disappointed in our emotional intelligence.

Every time our hands brush over a paint can or ladder, electricity hums under the noise of productivity, reminding us that pretending is exhausting and ultimately futile.

"You missed a spot," West says, pointing to the corner like he's trying to be professional and failing.

"Occupational hazard of working with someone who radiates judgment like it's a superpower," I shoot back, but there's no heat in it, only the familiar warmth that's been growing between us for weeks.

He snorts. "At least I'm consistent."

By noon, we're both covered in paint and pretending not to look at each other, pretending we don't keep catching each other's eyes and looking away like teenagers who've been caught holding hands.

Nonna brings sandwiches, eyes narrowed like she's gauging our vital signs and finding them wanting. "Eat," she commands. "Flirting burns calories, but emotional denial gives you wrinkles."

"We're not—" I start, but she's already gone, leaving us alone with sandwiches that suddenly feel like evidence.

We eat in silence until I can't stand it, until the weight of everything unsaid becomes heavier than the fear of saying it.

"About last night—"

"Shouldn't have happened," he says, too fast, like he's trying to convince himself. Then softer, like he can't help the truth: "But it did."

"Right," I force a laugh that sounds brittle, like it might break under pressure. "Professional boundaries. Safety first."

He looks at me for a long moment, eyes steady, voice careful. "Safety's relative."

Something tightens in my chest, like hope and fear are having a wrestling match. "You're infuriating."

"So I'm told."

I turn back to the wall before I say something that would need sanding later, something that would change everything again. He steps closer anyway, close enough that I can smell cedar and paint and the kind of danger that doesn't come with warning labels, the kind that feels like coming home.

"Luna—" he starts, but Moose barks from the doorway, saving us both, breaking the spell like the good boy he is.

"Lunch break over!" I announce too brightly, like I can shout away the tension. "Back to work!"

He shakes his head, smiling despite himself, and the smile reaches his eyes, crinkling the corners like he's actually, genuinely happy. "You're impossible."

"Occupational hazard," I echo, and this time the words feel like a promise, like an acknowledgment that this—whatever this is—is worth the risk.

By sunset, the inn gleams in all the places we managed to agree on, all the places we managed to create something beautiful together. My heart, less so. I sit on the porch steps after he leaves, watching the water turn to molten gold, and whisper to no one, to the ocean, to the universe, "I'm so doomed."

And I'm smiling when I say it, because doom has never felt so much like hope.

Today's Playlist:
"Caffeinated Denial" – Morning Lie Strategy
"Emotional Coup" – Heart Uprising
"Boundaries Are For Cowards" – Professional Hazard

Day 15 — West

I wake up before sunrise, which means either guilt or purpose has decided to win the morning. I'm not sure which is worse. Moose groans from the foot of the bed like he's filing a formal complaint about the early hour and my general life choices.

I pour coffee, stare at the deck blueprints, and tell myself it's not personal—it's just logistics. The supplier in town can't deliver decking boards for another week. I scroll through old contacts until I hit the name I don't want to call: Luis, an old coworker from Seattle who still owes me a favor from that time I covered his shift when his wife went into labor three weeks early.

He answers on the second ring, sounding way too cheerful for someone who's about to get dragged into my emotional construction mess. "Harding. Didn't think you did small talk or social calls."

"I don't," I say. "I need decking material. Redwood, pre-sealed. Two days."

A low whistle. "What's the emergency?"

"An inn," I say, and the word feels heavier than it should. "Deadline's tight."

"An inn," he repeats, and I can hear the smile in his voice, the knowing tone that says he sees right through me. "That code for someone you like?"

"It's code for work," I say, and ignore the smile in his voice, ignore the fact that I'm lying to myself and to him.

He laughs. "I'll see what I can do. But you owe me. Big time."

When I hang up, Moose tilts his head like he knows better, like he can smell the emotional turmoil coming off me in waves. "Don't start," I warn him. He yawns, smug and judgmental, like he's the wisest creature in this whole mess. "It's not charity," I add, mostly to convince myself. "It's efficiency. Professional networking."

But as I'm getting ready to head to the inn, my phone rings. It's Luna, and her voice sounds wrong - tight, panicked.

"West? You need to get here. Now."

"What's wrong? Is it..."

"Just come," she says, and hangs up.

I make it to the inn in record time, Moose already sensing that this isn't a normal workday. Luna meets me at the door, her face pale, her hands shaking.

"The basement," she says simply. "It's bad."

The moment I walk into the basement, I smell it - that musty, rotting smell that means trouble. The water isn't dripping anymore; it's flowing steadily from somewhere behind the main support beam for the east wing. The beam that's been holding up this part of the building for approximately 120 years. The beam that's now soaked through and starting to bow in a way that support beams are definitely not supposed to bow.

"Shit," I say to the empty basement. "Shit, shit, shit."

"How bad is it?" Luna asks, though she already knows the answer.

"Bad," I say, shining my flashlight on the damage. "This is going to stop all work on the east wing immediately. We need a structural engineer. This is... this is catastrophic."

She doesn't say anything for a long time, just stares at the water damage. I expect anger, or frustration, or at least some choice words about the state of New England construction.

Instead, she says, "My grandfather built this section himself."

I look at her. "What?"

"After the war," she says, running her hand along the damp concrete wall. "He came back and added the east wing. Said the inn was too small for all the stories it wanted to hold."

"Luna, I'm sorry, but..."

"No, it's okay." She takes a deep breath. "He would want us to fix it right. He was a craftsman. He believed in doing things properly, even when it was hard."

That afternoon, the structural engineer confirms our fears. His name is Dave and he looks exactly like you'd expect a structural engineer to look - slightly rumpled, very serious, and carrying a clipboard like it's a weapon of mass destruction.

"Well," Dave says after examining the damage for approximately three hours, "the good news is that this building has incredible bones. The bad news is that your main support beam has been slowly rotting for approximately forty years, and you're lucky it didn't collapse during the last snowstorm."

"Six weeks minimum," Dave says, not looking up from his calculations. "And that's if everything goes perfectly, which, let's be honest, it never does."

"Six weeks," Luna repeats, her voice hollow. "But Nonna's already booked guests for opening weekend."

When we tell Nonna, she doesn't look surprised or upset. She just looks... thoughtful.

"Your grandfather had the same problem when he built the east wing," she says finally. "Found water damage in the original foundation. Had to rebuild the entire thing. Took him three months."

She pulls out a dusty ledger. "This was your grandfather's. He kept track of every renovation, every repair. Right here. May 1978. 'Water damage to east foundation. Must rebuild. Timeline: three months. Cost: more than we have. Solution: work harder.'"

Luna takes the ledger, her fingers tracing her grandfather's handwriting. "Three months."

"Sometimes things have to break before they can be rebuilt properly," Nonna says, looking between us. "You'll figure it out. You always do."

Later that night, after Nonna has gone to bed, Luna finds me in the dining room, looking at the architectural drawings we made last week.

"I called the guests," she says quietly. "I refunded their money. Most of them were really understanding."

"What if we lose the magic, West? What if we fix the building but break the magic?"

I want to hug her. I want to tell her that magic doesn't come from buildings or timelines. I want to tell her that the magic is in the people who love the place enough to save it, even when it's hard and heartbreaking.

Instead, I say, "Your grandfather didn't lose the magic when he rebuilt the foundation. He made room for more of it."

Luna smiles, a real smile this time. "We're going to fix this, West."

"I know," I say. "Together."

The word hangs in the air between us, full of promise and possibility. Together. It feels like the beginning of something important.

At the inn, Luna's already painting the breakfast nook, her hair up in a messy bun that's clearly one paint smudge away from art. She's wearing my old flannel again. I tell myself it's coincidence that I forgot it on purpose, that I didn't leave it there like a breadcrumbs trail leading back to me.

"Morning," she says, too bright, too cheerful. The smile doesn't quite reach her eyes, like she's still processing the structural damage news, like we both are.

I pretend not to notice the tension that's still hanging between us like smoke. "Morning," I answer, setting down my tools with more force than necessary. "Deck order's being handled. We'll have the boards by Friday."

Her brush freezes mid-stroke. "What? How?"

"Called in a favor," I say, like it's no big deal, like I didn't just sacrifice my dignity for her roof deck.

"You..." she turns, blinking. "You called someone? You hate calling people. You consider phone calls to be a form of medieval torture."

"Desperation breeds networking," I deadpan, but my heart's doing something stupid and complicated behind my ribs.

Her lips twitch. "That's not networking. That's sorcery. You're basically a construction wizard now."

"Either way, it'll save the schedule," I say, trying to sound professional and failing.

Nonna appears like a benevolent hurricane, carrying a tray of cookies that smell like heaven and emotional manipulation. "You did a good thing," she tells me, eyes twinkling with that knowing look that says she sees everything, understands everything, and probably orchestrated half of it. "Kindness under protest is still kindness. And more romantic, if you ask me."

"I'm allergic to compliments," I mutter, because I am, because they feel too vulnerable.

"Then consider this medicine," she says, pressing a cookie into my hand with the precision of a nurse giving a shot. "And consider it a thank you from everyone who wants to see this inn succeed. Especially Luna."

Then she's gone again, mission accomplished, leaving me with a cookie and the uncomfortable feeling that I've just been thoroughly analyzed and approved.

Luna leans against the wall, watching me with those eyes that see too much. "Why would you do that?"

"It's my job," I say, because it's the safe answer, the true answer that doesn't tell the whole story.

She shakes her head, not buying it for a second. "Not the calling-in-favors part. The part where you care enough to fix something that's not your responsibility. The part where you're putting yourself out there for someone else's dream."

I shrug, trying to look casual while my heart is pounding like I've just run a marathon. "I like working with solid materials. Helps the rest make sense."

"That's not an answer," she says softly.

"Didn't sound like a question," I counter, but we both know I'm avoiding the real answer, avoiding the truth that's been growing between us like wildflowers through concrete.

She laughs, soft but genuine, and for a second the tension between us turns into something gentler, something warmer. Then Moose trots in, carrying a paint rag in triumph like he's just won the lottery or successfully stolen something important, and the moment splinters back into chaos.

"Your dog's a menace," she says, chasing him around the room like they're playing tag, like they've been doing this dance forever.

"He's a distraction," I correct, but I'm smiling, because I can't help it. "I pay him hourly in belly rubs and stolen paint rags."

The rest of the day unspools in quiet rhythm. She paints; I reinforce beams. Every now and then, she hums, and I let myself listen, let myself get lost in the sound of her happiness. When the truck pulls up that evening—Luis's delivery ahead of schedule, because apparently Luis is a better friend than I deserve—Luna's outside to meet it, her eyes going wide like it's Christmas morning.

She runs a hand over the boards like they're made of gold, like they're the most precious things she's ever seen. "You actually pulled it off."

I shrug, trying to play it cool while my heart is doing cartwheels. "Don't sound so surprised."

She looks at me for a long moment, and something unspoken moves between us, something heavy and important and terrifying. "You keep pretending you don't have a heart, but your actions keep disagreeing with you."

"Must be defective wiring," I say, because I'm a coward.

She smiles, and it's the kind of smile that could change the world, or at least my world. "Then don't fix it."

We unload the boards in silence, the kind that hums instead of hurts, the kind that feels like we're building something more than just a roof deck.

Later, when I get home, Luis texts: "She's special, huh? You're welcome."

I don't answer. But Moose nudges my knee like he already knows, like he approves, like he's been Team Luna from day one.

Tomorrow, I tell myself, I'll keep my distance. I'll be professional. I'll remember that I have a job waiting in Seattle, a life that doesn't involve coastal inns and women who name paint colors and grandmothers who see everything.

Moose snores. He doesn't believe me. Neither do I.

Today's Playlist:

"Construction Wizard" – Decking Sorcery

"Kindness Under Protest" – Romantic Logistics

"Defective Wiring" – Heart Malfunction

Day 14 — Luna

The morning light on the roof deck feels different—like it knows it's being saved, like it understands that something important is happening up here, something more than just construction and renovation. I climb the last set of stairs and find West already there, crouched over blueprints, pencil tucked behind his ear like he's been up for hours, like he couldn't stay away from this project, from me.

Moose sprawls beside him, a loyal audience of one, occasionally sighing like he's providing emotional support through dramatic breathing.

"You're early," I say, setting down two coffees like they're peace offerings in the ongoing war between my heart and my brain.

"So are you," he says without looking up, like he's not surprised to see me, like he was expecting me. "Guess we're both bad at pretending this place doesn't own us."

I glance over his shoulder and realize what he's doing. The layout's changed—he's shifted the rail supports, widened the seating area, and rerouted the drainage so the deck stays intact. My deck. My dream, being improved by his practical expertise and his surprising understanding of what matters.

"You know," I say, studying the blueprints, "for someone who claims not to understand my artistic vision, you're doing a pretty good job of interpreting it."

West looks up, and there's a smile playing at the corners of his mouth. "I understand more than you think I do. You want this space to feel like it's suspended between ocean and sky. You want people to sit up here and feel like they're part of something bigger than themselves."

I stare at him. "How did you..."

"Because I know you," he says softly. "Even when you were seventeen, you were always looking for the magic in things. Always

89

trying to find the spaces where ordinary life touched something extraordinary."

That's when I get an idea. Something that probably won't work but feels important anyway. "Teach me."

"Teach you what?"

"This," I say, gesturing to the blueprints, to the tools, to the world he moves through with such easy confidence. "Teach me how to do something real. Something practical. Something I can point to and say 'I made that.'"

West considers this, his expression unreadable. "You're a writer, Luna. You make stories. That's pretty real."

"But I can't hold them," I say, and my voice sounds more vulnerable than I intended. "I can't touch them. I want to make something with my hands. Something that exists even when the power goes out."

He studies me for a long moment, then nods slowly. "Okay. But you have to promise to listen to my instructions. No creative interpretations, no 'I think this would look better if...' Just following directions."

"I promise," I say, even though we both know I'm terrible at following directions.

That's how I end up spending the next hour learning to use a circular saw. West is a patient teacher, explaining angles and measurements and safety procedures with the kind of thoroughness that suggests he's taught this before. Probably to people who were better students than me.

"Your grip is too tight," he says, adjusting my hands on the saw. "You're holding it like you're afraid it's going to bite you. Relax. Let the tool do the work."

My hands are shaking, and I'm hyperaware of how close he's standing, how his arms brush against mine as he demonstrates the proper technique. Focus, Luna. Focus on the wood, not on the man who smells like sawdust and coffee and everything you've ever wanted.

"Like this?" I ask, my voice squeaking slightly.

"Perfect," he says, but he doesn't move away. "Now, slow and steady. Don't rush it."

I take a deep breath and guide the saw through the piece of wood he's clamped down. For a second, it feels like it's going to go wrong, like I'm going to mess it up, but then the cut smooths out and I'm actually doing it. I'm actually cutting a straight line.

"See?" West says, and I can hear the pride in his voice. "You can do this."

We spend the next hour like that - him teaching, me learning, the both of us falling into an easy rhythm that feels older than time. He shows me how to measure properly, how to sand without leaving marks, how to read the grain of the wood. I'm clumsy at first, making mistakes, getting frustrated, but he's patient with me, encouraging, never making me feel stupid for not knowing things he's known his whole life.

"You're a good teacher," I say, after I successfully complete a small project - a simple wooden box that's supposed to hold mail or magazines or whatever people need to hold.

"You're a good student," he counters, but he's smiling. "When you're not trying to redesign the project halfway through."

"That was one time," I protest, but I'm laughing too.

"There's sawdust in your hair," he says, reaching out to brush it away. His fingers linger against my cheek, and suddenly the easy rhythm between us shifts into something else, something charged and electric.

"West," I whisper, and my voice is shaking.

"Yeah?"

"I think..." I start, but I don't know how to finish. I think I'm falling in love with you all over again. I think this moment is more intimate than any kiss we've shared. I think watching you teach me something, seeing the patience in your eyes and the pride in your smile, is making me feel things I wasn't prepared to feel.

He seems to understand what I'm trying to say. "I know," he says softly. "Me too."

We stand there for a long time, surrounded by the tools of his trade, the smell of sawdust filling the air, the small wooden box on the workbench between us - tangible proof that I made something real, that I can learn this world he lives in, that maybe our two worlds aren't as different as I thought.

"Can we make another one?" I ask finally.

West smiles. "What did you have in mind?"

"Something bigger," I say. "Something that matters."

"Everything we build together matters," he says, and the way he looks at me makes me believe it's true.

Today's Playlist: "The Builder" by Foo Fighters, "Handyman" by The Dandy Warhols, "I'll Be There for You" by The Rembrandts

"You said the roof deck was inefficient," I say, trying to sound casual and failing spectacularly.

"It is," he sketches another line, and his hand moves with such confidence, such certainty. "But so are you."

I blink. "Is that an insult or a compliment?"

He shrugs, like he doesn't care, but I can see the hint of a smile playing around his mouth. "Depends who's asking."

The corner of my mouth twitches. "You're adjusting the plan. You're changing the design based on what I said."

He exhales through his nose, like he's annoyed that I noticed, that I called him on it. "You were right. It's the heart of the place. People fall in love up here." He pauses, and his voice softens. "Not everyone."

"Not everyone knows how," I say, and immediately wish I could swallow the words, because they reveal too much, because they sound like vulnerability.

He studies me like he's measuring load-bearing truth, like he's trying to understand the architecture of my heart. "Then maybe we remind them."

The silence that follows isn't heavy. It's warm, like sunlight through salt air, like possibility. I sit beside him and hand over his coffee. He takes it, careful not to touch my fingers, and fails spectacularly.

Nonna appears at the top of the stairs with the grace of a retired general and a tray of pastries that smell like heaven and probably contain some kind of love potion. "Breakfast," she announces. "And unsolicited wisdom: do not underestimate the strength of a roof—or a woman who insists on keeping one."

She sets the tray down and disappears before either of us can respond, leaving behind the scent of baked goods and strategic emotional meddling.

"She's terrifying," West mutters, but there's affection in his voice.

"She's effective," I grin. "You two would get along. You could bond over your shared love of being right and your mutual fear of showing emotions."

We eat on the deck edge, watching the sunlight chase across the bay like it's painting the world just for us. When we finish, we measure beam spacing, mark joist lines, and argue about railing angles. Every time his hand brushes mine, the argument loses momentum, like neither of us wants to fight when we could be touching.

"You always this stubborn?" he asks, aligning a post with the precision of someone who measures twice and cuts once.

"Only when I'm right," I say, because we both know I am.

"Good," he says, and there's warmth in his voice. "Keeps me honest."

By noon, the deck's skeleton starts to take shape, looking less like a construction project and more like a promise, like something real and lasting. He stands, stretching his back, eyes scanning the horizon like he's trying to memorize it, like he's afraid he might forget this moment.

"You'll get your view," he says quietly, and his voice is rough with emotion. "Even if it kills the timeline."

"You don't have to do that," I say, my throat tight.

"I know," he says, and the simple words carry more weight than any grand declaration.

I don't thank him right away. Gratitude feels too small for what he just did, too inadequate for the way he's changing everything. Instead, I pick up a paint can and my marker. The label reads: "Day 14 — Blueprints and Heartbeats."

He catches it and smirks, and it's the real thing this time, no hiding it. "Accurate."

"See?" I say, smiling because I can't help it. "Even inefficiency has rhythm."

When he leaves to grab supplies, I stay behind a little longer, tracing the fresh lumber with my fingertips. The boards are cool, solid, real. This place is starting to remember what it feels like to be wanted, to be loved. And so am I.

Today's Playlist:

"Roof Deck Heart" – Structural Romance

"Strategic Emotional Meddling" – Nonna's Pastries

"Measure Twice, Fall Once" – Construction Love Logic

Day 13 — West

The roof deck hums beneath us like it's alive, like it's singing a song only we can hear. Night has settled soft and slow, wrapping the inn in the scent of cedar and salt and something else, something new and fragile and terrifying.

We've been working since dawn, but neither of us is ready to leave, neither of us is ready to break the spell that's been weaving itself around us all day. Luna sits on the railing, hair loose, paint on her wrist like a secret only I'm allowed to read. She laughs at something small—a crooked board, a gull dive-bombing the dumpster, the way Moose is snoring in rhythm with the waves—and it lands in my chest like oxygen, like it's the first real breath I've taken in years.

"Tomorrow we stain the railing," I say, mostly to keep talking, mostly to convince myself that there will be a tomorrow, that this won't end tonight.

She grins, and her smile is like sunlight breaking through storm clouds. "Tomorrow we breathe."

The light from the window spills between us, warm and uneven, painting her in gold and shadows that make her look like something out of a dream. I catch myself tracing the line of her jaw, the curve of her mouth, and I should look away, I should stop, I should maintain some semblance of control, but I can't.

"I should probably head out," I say, but neither of us moves. "Early start tomorrow."

"Right," Luna says, but she slides off the railing and moves closer instead. "Early starts and responsible adult decisions."

Her fingers brush against mine, and electricity shoots up my arm like we're wiring the building and ourselves at the same time. "West?"

"Yeah?"

"Why did you really come back to Harbor Street?"

The question catches me off guard. I thought we were doing this dance - the light flirting, the careful distance, the moments that feel like everything and nothing all at once. I wasn't prepared for honesty.

I lean against the railing, looking out at the dark ocean. "After my dad died, I sort of... drifted. Moved around from job to job, city to city. Never stayed anywhere long enough to put down roots."

"Because you were running?"

"Because I was lost," I correct gently. "There's a difference. Running is when you're trying to escape something. Being lost is when you're trying to find something."

I can feel her watching me, waiting for the rest of the story.

"I ended up in Seattle for a while. Good work, decent money, nice apartment. But it felt... wrong. Like wearing someone else's clothes." I pause, remembering the loneliness of that year. "One day I was at this hardware store, buying supplies for a job, and I overheard these two guys talking about their hometowns. One of them mentioned Harbor Street, said something about how the inn was struggling, how Nonna was getting older."

I look at Luna then. "I packed my bags that night. Drove for three days straight. Didn't even call ahead."

"Why?"

"Because I was tired of being lost," I say quietly. "And I thought... maybe if I came back to where I started, I could find my way back to myself."

"And did you?" she asks, her voice soft.

"I found Moose," I say with a small smile. "And I found this workshop. And I found some kind of routine that feels like peace."

"But?"

"But I didn't feel... whole," I admit, and the words are scary but true. "It was like missing a piece of a puzzle and not knowing what the piece was supposed to look like."

Luna steps closer, until there's barely any space between us. "And now?"

"Now I think maybe the piece was always supposed to be you," I say, and the confession hangs in the air between us, raw and terrifying and completely honest.

Her breath catches. "West..."

"I've loved you since we were seventeen," I continue, because once you start telling the truth, it's hard to stop. "Since that chemistry class where you helped me understand electron configurations by comparing them to dance partners. Since the way you'd bite your lip when you were concentrating. Since the way you looked at me like you saw past all the walls I'd built around myself."

I take her hand. "When you left for Boston, I thought about following you. Packed a bag twice, even looked at apartments online. But I knew that wouldn't be fair to you. You needed to find your own way, without me complicating things."

"Complicating things?" she whispers.

"I love you enough to let you go," I say. "But I also love you enough to wait for you to come back."

Tears are streaming down her face now, and I gently wipe them away with my thumb. "I'm not going anywhere, Luna."

"You say that now," she says, her voice trembling.

"I've been saying it for ten years," I say. "Every day, since the moment you left."

She leans in then, and I think she's going to kiss me. I want her to kiss me. I've wanted her to kiss me since we were teenagers sitting on this same roof, talking about dreams and futures that somehow led us back to this moment.

But at the last second, she pulls back. "I can't," she whispers. "Not yet. I need to be sure this is real, that I'm choosing this for the right reasons."

I nod, because I understand. "I'm not going anywhere," I say again. "I'll wait."

"Thank you," she says, and it sounds like both a beginning and an ending.

After she goes inside, I stay on the roof for a long time, looking at the stars, thinking about how love isn't always about grand gestures or dramatic moments. Sometimes it's about patience. Sometimes it's about being the person who waits. Sometimes it's about loving someone enough to let them find their way back to you on their own terms.

Moose appears at the top of the stairs, tail wagging like he's been waiting for me. "Yeah, buddy," I say, scratching behind his ears. "Let's go home."

But as I walk back to my truck, I realize that for the first time in ten years, I don't feel like I'm waiting anymore. I feel like I'm exactly where I'm supposed to be.

Today's Playlist: "The Reason" by Hoobastank, "Here Without You" by 3 Doors Down, "I Don't Want to Miss a Thing" by Aerosmith

"You keep staring like you're waiting for permission," she murmurs, and her voice is soft, like she's afraid to break the moment.

"Maybe I am," I admit, and the words feel dangerous, like I'm crossing a line I can't uncross.

She steps closer, barefoot, careful on the deck that's still rough in places. Her fingers brush the edge of my tool belt, an accidental touch that feels anything but, like electricity running up my spine like a warning and a promise all at once.

The world contracts to that single point of contact—wood creaking, her breath catching, my heartbeat trying to outrun itself like it knows something I don't.

"West," she says, and my name sounds different here—softer, riskier, like she's testing the weight of it, like she's seeing if it can hold everything we're feeling.

I move before I can think better of it, before I can talk myself out of it, before I can remember all the reasons this is a terrible idea. The kiss is inevitable—weeks of tension, all the unsaid things collapsing at once like a building demolition, but this isn't destruction, it's creation.

It's hungry and patient, clumsy and certain, like we're learning each other's language in real time. Her hands find my shoulders; mine memorize the small of her back, the curve of her waist, the way she fits against me like we were designed to be together. The air tastes like rain and something sweeter I can't name, something that tastes like hope and home and everything I've been searching for without knowing what I was looking for.

When we finally break, she leans her forehead against mine, and we're both breathing hard, like we've just run a marathon, like we've just survived something important.

"That was—" she starts, but she's laughing, and the sound is shaky and beautiful.

"Terrible idea," I finish, because it's true, because I'm leaving in thirteen days, because she deserves someone who stays, someone who doesn't have baggage in Seattle and a history of running.

"Best kind," she whispers, and her lips brush mine again, soft and certain.

I laugh, low and unsteady, because she's right, because this feels more real than anything I've ever known. "You're trouble."

"Efficient trouble," she counters, and I can feel her smile against my mouth.

We stand there, breath tangled, neither ready to let go, neither ready to face what comes next. She rests her head against my chest, and for a moment the world feels built right, like everything has finally clicked into place, like I've finally found my way home.

Later, when she drifts to sleep beside me on the couch downstairs, the ocean keeps time against the windows, steady and rhythmic like it's been keeping this beat forever, waiting for us to find our way to it. I watch the ceiling and know there's no blueprint for this, no plan, no schedule.

Somewhere between blueprints and skin, I lost the plan. Or maybe I finally found it.

Today's Playlist:
"Deck Song" – Cedar Symphony
"Permission Staring" – Dangerous Observations
"Structure and Surrender" – Blueprint of the Heart

Day 12 — Luna

The morning smells like coffee, sawdust, and something new that doesn't have a name yet, something that feels like hope and possibility and the kind of change that terrifies and excites me all at once. I wake on the couch, wrapped in West's flannel and the steady hush of rain outside, and for one dizzy minute, I forget about the bank, the deadlines, the thirty days that felt like a life sentence when I arrived and now feel like not nearly enough time.

I just remember his heartbeat under my ear and the way the world finally felt like it fit, like I'd been searching for the missing piece my whole life and found it in the arms of a grumpy contractor with a dog who's a better matchmaker than most dating apps.

The kettle whistles. West is already in the kitchen, sleeves rolled, pretending to read the supply ledger like he wasn't just sleeping beside me, like we didn't just change everything between us. He doesn't look up when I stretch and yawn, but I can feel the tension in his shoulders, the careful way he's holding himself.

"Morning," I say softly, testing the waters, testing this new territory we've stumbled into.

"Morning," he says, his tone steady, neutral—the sound of walls going back up, of distance being carefully reconstructed like the framing we've been working on together.

He pours two mugs, slides one toward me. "We've got a lot to do today."

Translation: We're not talking about last night. We're not talking about the kiss or the couch or the way he held me like I was something precious, something worth protecting. My chest aches anyway.

"Then we should start early," I say, playing along because I have to, because this is still a job and there are still deadlines and I'm not brave enough to demand more, not yet.

101

Before I can find the courage to tease him back to easy ground, to the comfortable rhythm we've established over weeks of working together, my phone buzzes across the counter like an angry insect demanding attention. The caller ID makes my stomach twist like I've just swallowed broken glass: First Harbor Bank.

I take it into the office, heart thudding in stereo against my ribs and the memory of his touch. "Ms. Castellano," says the voice I've learned to dread, the voice that represents everything standing between us and this dream. "Just checking on progress. The extension expires in eighteen days. We'll need verified completion photos and an inspection report before disbursing the next installment."

"Of course," I say, cheerful in the way only panic can sound, like I'm not standing here with the ghost of his kiss still on my lips, like my entire world didn't just tilt on its axis. "We're right on schedule."

When I hang up, I stare at the invoices spread across the desk—timelines, receipts, a thousand tiny pieces of proof that we're actually doing this, that we're actually making this dream real. Outside, hammers and rain argue rhythmically, like they're having their own conversation about time and pressure and the things that build up and break down.

West finds me a few minutes later, leaning in the doorway like he's afraid to get too close, like he's not sure which version of me he's going to find. "Bad call?"

"Just the bank," I say, trying to sound casual and failing. "Reminding me the universe runs on deadlines and doesn't care about romance."

He leans against the doorframe, arms folded like he's building his own walls, his own defenses. "We'll make it."

"You sound sure," I say, because I need to hear it, because I need someone to believe this is possible when I'm suddenly not so sure.

"I have to be," he says, and there's something in his voice, something heavy and important.

Nonna appears, armed with a pan of muffins and unsolicited optimism, like she's been timing this entrance perfectly. "Eat," she orders, setting down muffins that smell like comfort and determination. "No one negotiates well on an empty stomach."

She glances between us, eyes narrowed like she can smell both tension and the awkward aftermath of emotional breakthroughs. "Also, never answer the phone during breakfast. Bad energy. Bad juju. Very Italian superstition, but also just common sense."

West hides a smile behind his coffee, and for a second I see the man I've been falling for, the man behind the walls. I throw him a glare I don't mean at all.

We spend the day in motion—me sanding trim, him checking wiring, both pretending the silence between us isn't saying more than words could. Every time I pass the window, the rain's eased, but the clouds still hang low, heavy with warning, like the sky is mirroring my own emotional weather system.

By afternoon, I've made a decision. "We're hosting a preview night," I announce, trying to sound more confident than I feel.

West looks up from the blueprint, confused. "A what?"

"A soft opening for locals. One night only. Photos, food, proof of progress. The bank needs to see life here, not numbers." I pause. "They need to see what we're building."

He studies me for a long moment, and the hint of a smile tugs at his mouth. "That's... ambitious."

"Ambitious is free," I say. "And we're fresh out of money."

He nods slowly, and I can see him weighing it, considering it. "Then I guess we'd better make it beautiful."

I exhale, some mix of fear and hope catching on the way out. "Beautiful and bank approved."

Nonna claps once from the kitchen, like she's been waiting for this exact moment. "I heard that! Add wine to the list. Banks love wine. Everyone loves wine. Wine solves everything."

I grin, jotting it down, and catch West watching me—something steady and quiet behind his eyes, something that looks like pride, like partnership, like maybe, just maybe, we're in this together for real.

Today's Playlist:

"Couch Confessions" – Morning After Logic

"Bank Dread" – Financial Anxiety Blues

"Ambitious Is Free" – Preview Night Dreams

Day 11 — West

Morning light cuts through the workshop in thin, merciless lines, like it's trying to expose all the things I've been trying to hide from myself. I'm halfway through checking voltage when my phone buzzes across the sawhorse like an angry hornet. Seattle. Again. Same number that's been haunting my pocket for three weeks, like a ghost that refuses to accept it's dead.

I stare at it long enough for Moose to huff like even he's tired of my indecision, like he can't believe I'm still pretending this is a choice I have to make. I pick up, because sometimes silence feels like surrender, because sometimes you have to face the thing you're running from.

"Harding," a voice says—bright, professional, already halfway across the continent and a lifetime away from here. "We need your answer. Project starts in ten days. Same rate plus bonus for early completion. You in?"

Ten days. I glance at the calendar tacked to the wall: eighteen left on the Castellano clock, seven before Luna's ridiculous preview night that somehow feels both impossible and inevitable. I can almost hear her voice: 'Ambitious is free,' and I wonder if that applies to life choices too.

"I'll call you back," I say, and hang up before the word yes can betray me, before I can say something I'll spend the rest of my life regretting.

Luna finds me in the workshop about an hour later. I'm trying to focus on rebuilding an old window frame, but my hands keep shaking, and the measurements aren't coming out right. Seattle is calling to me with the promise of everything I thought I wanted - good money, challenging projects, the validation of being wanted by people who don't know my history or my heart.

"Tough morning?" she asks, leaning against the doorframe.

"Tough life," I correct, not looking up from my work.

105

She comes closer, studying the window frame I'm supposed to be rebuilding. "That's not going to work."

"What?"

"Your measurements are off by half an inch," she says, pointing. "And you're using the wrong kind of wood for this period. This is pine, but the original frames were probably oak or at least a hardwood."

I drop my tools. "How do you know that?"

"Research," she says simply. "I've been reading about historic preservation. About how buildings like this were constructed. About what materials they used."

Something tightens in my chest. "You're researching preservation?"

"Someone has to," she says, and there's an edge to her voice that I haven't heard before. "This isn't just about making it look pretty, West. This is about honoring the history, about respecting what this place has been and what it could be again."

I lean against the workbench, suddenly exhausted. "Luna, what are we doing here?"

"We're renovating an inn," she says, like it's the most obvious thing in the world.

"No, I mean... what are we doing?" I gesture between us. "This thing between us. This... tension. These moments that feel like everything and nothing all at once."

She considers this for a moment. "I think we're building something."

"A building?"

"A foundation," she says quietly. "For whatever comes next."

The workshop is quiet except for the sound of breathing - mine, hers, Moose's soft snores from the corner. Outside, I can hear the sounds of Harbor Street waking up, the familiar rhythm of a town that's been my home longer than anywhere else.

"Seattle called again," I admit.

Luna doesn't look surprised. "And?"

"They want me for a big project. Ten days start time. Good money."

"And what did you say?"

"That I'd call them back." I look at her, really look at her, at the woman who came back into my life and turned it completely upside down. "What should I say?"

"That's not my decision to make," she says gently.

"Isn't it?" I challenge. "You're the one who came back. You're the one who's making this place feel like... like it could be something again."

Luna walks over to the pile of wood I've been sorting through. She runs her hand over a piece of oak, testing its grain, its strength. "You know, when I was in Boston, I thought I knew what success looked like. I thought it was a byline in a major publication, a fancy apartment, a life that looked good on Instagram."

She looks up at me. "But I was wrong. Success isn't about what other people think of your life. It's about whether you can look at yourself in the mirror and know you're being honest about who you are and what you want."

"So what do you want, Luna?"

"I want to finish this inn," she says, and her voice is firm, certain. "I want to write stories that matter. I want to wake up in the morning and feel like I'm exactly where I'm supposed to be."

"And where is that?"

Her eyes meet mine, and the air between us crackles with all the unspoken words, all the years of wanting and waiting and wondering. "That's the question, isn't it?"

Instead of answering, I pick up the oak plank she was touching. "You're right about the wood. Oak would be better for this frame. More durable, more authentic to the period."

I start measuring the oak, my hands steady now, the shaking gone. Luna watches me work, and something shifts between us, something settles.

"West?"

"Yeah?"

"If you stay," she says, her voice barely above a whisper, "we could make this amazing. The inn, the town, us."

I stop measuring and look at her. Really look at her. At the writer who came home to find herself, at the woman who sees the magic in old buildings and tired towns, at the person who's been quietly changing my life without even trying.

"If I stay," I say, my voice thick with emotion, "it won't be for the inn or the town."

Luna's breath catches. "Then why?"

"Because you came back," I say simply. "And I'm tired of missing you."

The words hang in the air between us, raw and honest and terrifyingly true. This isn't just about renovations or deadlines or career choices anymore. This is about choosing. This is about taking a chance on something that might break us or might save us.

"That's a really good reason," Luna says softly.

"I thought so too."

We work in silence for a while after that, measuring and cutting and fitting pieces of oak together like we're building something new from something old. And maybe we are. Maybe that's what love is - not finding something perfect, but taking something broken and beautiful and real and choosing to build with it anyway.

Today's Playlist: "The Reason" by Hoobastank, "Homesick" by Kings of Leon, "I Won't Give Up" by Jason Mraz

The inn hums around me—sawdust and sunlight, the smell of coffee drifting from the kitchen like an invitation I'm trying to resist. Luna's laugh carries down the hall—bright, determined, stubbornly optimistic. I tell myself to focus on measurements, but the line of her voice reroutes every plan I have, every logical argument I've been making about why I should go back to Seattle, why I should choose the safe path, the predictable one.

She bursts through the doorway holding a paint swatch like it's a lottery ticket she just won. "Tell me this isn't perfect."

I take it. Soft gray with a hint of blue, the color of sky just before sunrise, the color of her eyes when she's happy. "It's fine."

"Fine?" she asks, like I've just insulted her child or her favorite playlist.

"It's more than fine," I admit, because I can't lie to her, because lying to her feels like lying to myself. "It's... calm."

Her smile widens, and it's like the sun came out specifically to make my life more complicated. "Calm is good. We could use calm."

She catches me looking at her and adds, teasing, like she knows exactly what she's doing to me, "Unless you've got better plans."

I don't answer. Not out loud.

By noon she's knee-deep in decorations for the preview night, humming something that sounds like courage and hope and all the things I'm trying to run from. I patch drywall and pretend not to watch, pretend I'm not memorizing the way she moves, the way she bites her lip when she's concentrating, the way she's making this place, this life, feel like home.

Every so often, she asks my opinion, and every time I pretend to be annoyed that she wants it, that she values my input, that she sees me as more than just a contractor.

Nonna shows up midafternoon with lemonade and interrogation like she's been training for this moment her entire life. "You look like a man about to leave and hating himself for it," she says, like she's reading my soul like it's a cheap paperback.

"Do I?" I ask, trying to sound offended and failing spectacularly.

She eyes me like she's built a lie detector out of intuition and eighty years of watching people make terrible life choices. "Leaving before the paint dries means you never see the color you made."

She pats my arm, gentle but firm, like she's delivering a message from the universe. "Don't be a fool, ragazzo. Fools have the cleanest suitcases and the emptiest rooms."

I don't have an answer for that. She leaves me with the lemonade and a headache shaped like truth, like the realization that I've been standing at a crossroads and pretending I'm just walking down a straight path.

By dusk, Luna's on the deck stringing lights that don't want to cooperate, like they're mirroring my own resistance to this thing between us. I climb up to help, mostly because I can't not, mostly because the thought of her struggling up there alone feels wrong.

Our fingers brush over the same cord; she laughs, that bright sound that makes everything else feel manageable, like with her here, anything is possible. "See?" she says. "Magic."

"Electrical hazard," I reply, but I'm smiling, because she's right, because this feels like magic.

"Same thing," she says, and we both know it's true.

Later, when she goes inside to check the oven, I pull my phone out again. The screen glows in the dim light—one new message: "Need your confirmation by tomorrow, West. The team's waiting."

I type a reply. Delete it. Type it again. Delete that too. Moose nudges my leg like he knows what indecision smells like, like he can smell the fear and hope battling it out in my heart.

I set the phone face down on the railing. The lights flicker on across the deck, warm and steady, illuminating the space we've created together, illuminating the choice I've been avoiding.

Luna's laugh drifts through the open door. I take a breath that feels like a choice, feels like stepping off a cliff and trusting there's something there to catch me.

Not today. Seattle can wait. Luna can't.

I type one last message: "Thanks, but I'm staying." Then I turn off my phone, because for the first time in years, I know exactly what I want, and it's not in Seattle.

Today's Playlist:
"Seattle Ghost" – Ringing Regrets
"Lemonade Truth" – Nonna's Wisdom
"Magic or Hazard" – Electrical Romance

Day 10 — Luna

The morning light feels like a dare. I wake to the sound of hammering and the smell of coffee, and for one dizzying minute, I forget about the preview night, about the bank, about the thirty days that feel like both a countdown and a lifeline.

Then I remember last night—West on the roof with the lights, the way he looked at me like he was seeing something he'd been searching for, the way the air between us felt charged with possibility, with the kind of electricity that doesn't come from wiring.

I make coffee and tell myself to focus on the practical—final decorations, final touches, final everything. But my hands keep shaking, and I know it's not just caffeine, it's hope, it's terror, it's the knowledge that tonight everything changes, tonight we either succeed or fail, tonight we find out if this dream is strong enough to hold.

West appears in the kitchen, looking rumpled and gorgeous, like he slept in his clothes or maybe he didn't sleep at all. His hair is a mess, his shirt is wrinkled, and his eyes are doing that thing where they're trying to hide behind walls that are clearly crumbling.

"You're late," I say, trying to sound casual and failing spectacularly.

"You're early," he counters, but there's no bite in it, just the familiar warmth that's been growing between us like wildflowers through concrete.

I slide a mug toward him. "Coffee?"

"Please." He takes it, his fingers brushing mine. The contact sends sparks up my arm like live wires, like the building itself is responding to this thing between us, to this connection that feels older and deeper than either of us.

"So," I say, trying to sound businesslike and mostly failing. "Final inspection is at three. Preview at seven. We have twelve hours to make this place look like it wasn't built on panic and caffeine."

112

"We can do it," he says, and the confidence in his voice is enough to make me believe it, enough to make me believe anything is possible when he's around.

Later that morning, I find Nonna in the garden, kneeling among the rose bushes with a pair of pruning shears that look older than I am. She's humming something that sounds vaguely like Sinatra, and for a moment, I can see the young woman she must have been - vibrant, beautiful, with the whole world ahead of her.

"Need help?" I ask, kneeling beside her.

Nonna looks up, her eyes crinkling at the corners. "These roses have been here since your grandfather and I bought this place. He planted them the week we got married. Said even an inn needs romance."

She cuts off a dead branch with practiced precision. "This one always struggles. Same spot every year. But if you're patient, if you give it what it needs, it comes back stronger."

We work in silence for a while, the familiar rhythm of pruning and tidying. I've missed this - working with my hands, being close to Nonna, the quiet satisfaction of making something beautiful.

"You know," Nonna says, not looking at me, "when we first bought this place, people thought we were crazy."

"Why?"

"It was a wreck," she says with a small smile. "Your grandfather had just come home from the war, I was pregnant with your mother, and we sank everything we had into this falling-down building. My father told me I was throwing my life away."

"What did you say?"

"I said I'd rather be poor with him than rich without him." She pauses, touching a rosebud with gentle fingers. "Your grandfather had this dream - not just an inn, but a place where people could come and find themselves again. He said the best stories happen in places that feel like home."

She looks at me then, and her eyes are full of tears. "He died two months before you were born. Never got to see you, never got to see this place full of guests again."

I put my arm around her. "Nonna..."

"He would have loved you so much," she says, her voice thick with emotion. "You have his spirit, you know. That stubborn belief that things can be better than they are. That love is worth fighting for."

We sit there for a long time, surrounded by roses and memories. I realize I've never really asked Nonna about her life before the inn, about the girl who fell in love with a soldier and risked everything for a dream.

"What was he like?" I ask softly. "Grandpa."

Nonna's face transforms. "Oh, Luna. He was... everything. Funny and kind and so brave, but also so gentle. He could fix anything, you know? Broken appliances, broken hearts, broken dreams. He just had this way of looking at things and seeing what they could be, not just what they were."

She wipes her eyes with the back of her hand. "When he got back from the war, he was different. Quieter. The war took something from him, something he never talked about. But this place..." She gestures toward the inn. "This place healed him. Giving other people a place to rest and recover... it healed him too."

I think about West, about the quiet way he moves through the world, about the careful precision with which he works. About the sadness in his eyes sometimes when he thinks no one is looking.

"Is that why you're so invested in West and me?" I ask gently.

Nonna looks surprised, then thoughtful. "Your grandfather saw people. Really saw them. He saw the girl working behind the counter at the grocery store who was secretly writing poetry. He saw the veteran who sat alone at the bar every night because he couldn't bear crowds. He saw me, when I was just a scared girl with too many dreams and not enough courage."

She smiles. "West sees you, Luna. He sees the real you, not the Boston writer or the prodigal daughter or any of the other labels people try to put on you. And you... you see him too."

"Nonna, I..."

"Shhh." She puts a finger on my lips. "You don't have to figure it all out right now. Just... let yourself be seen. That's the hardest part, isn't it? Letting someone see all the pieces you try so hard to hide."

Later that night, I find the old photo album Nonna mentioned. It's in the attic, covered in dust and memories. Inside are pictures of my grandparents as young people - my grandfather in his uniform, my grandmother with her hair in victory rolls, both of them impossibly young and full of hope.

There's a picture of them standing in front of the inn when it was still a wreck, their arms around each other, smiling like they had all the secrets of the universe. And beneath it, in my grandmother's neat handwriting, is a caption:

"Starting forever. October 12, 1946."

I sit there in the attic, surrounded by history, and realize that this inn isn't just a building. It's a love story, written in wood and plaster and determination. And somehow, impossibly, I'm writing the next chapter.

Nonna appears like she's been summoned by the sound of optimism, like she can sense hope from three rooms away. She's wearing her good apron and the kind of expression that says she's been planning this victory lap her entire life. "The kitchen is ready. The wine is breathing. The gossip network has been activated. This town will show up for you, bambina."

She glances between us, eyes twinkling like she knows exactly what happened on the roof last night, like she can smell the emotional breakthrough and the fact that we're both pretending nothing changed when everything changed. "Also, I made extra cannoli. Because celebrations require cannoli. It's Italian law."

By noon, the inn looks like a dream—rooms painted and staged, lights strung, decorations arranged with the kind of care that feels like love, like hope. West moves through the space like he belongs here, like he's been part of this story all along, and I realize with a jolt that he has been, that he's been as essential to this renovation as the nails and paint, as the dreams and determination.

The inspector arrives at three exactly, a man named Dave who looks like he's seen too many renovations and trusts none of them. He moves through the rooms with the slow, careful eye of someone who knows what to look for, who knows how buildings fail.

At first, it's good. He nods at the wiring, checks the outlets, runs his hands over the railing like he's testing its integrity, its strength. I hold my breath and hope, because this is it, this is the moment everything changes.

Then he gets to the roof deck.

"Interesting choice," he says, looking at the deck, at the view, at the way we've arranged the space to capture the light, to frame the ocean like it's a painting. "But the drainage isn't up to code."

My heart drops like a stone. "What?"

"The slope needs to be adjusted by at least two degrees," he says, like it's a simple thing, like it's not a death sentence. "And the railing spacing is off by half an inch."

West steps forward, his voice calm, steady. "We can fix that."

Dave shakes his head. "Not by tonight. You'll need to reschedule."

"No," I say, and the word comes out fierce, like I'm drawing a line in the sand, like I'm refusing to let this dream die because of two degrees and half an inch. "Tonight."

Dave looks at me, then at West, and there's something like respect in his eyes, like he recognizes the stubborn determination that's gotten us this far. "You have until six. Then I come back."

He leaves, and for a minute we just stand there, the silence heavy with the weight of his words, with the challenge he's thrown down.

"Well," West says finally, and there's something like excitement in his voice, like he thrives on this kind of pressure, like he was born for moments like this. "Guess we're not done yet."

"No," I agree, and my heart is pounding with adrenaline and something else, something that feels like trust, like partnership. "We're not."

We work like people possessed—West adjusting the deck slope, me recalibrating the railing spacing, both of us moving with the kind of efficiency that only comes from desperation, from knowing that failure is not an option.

By five-thirty, we're done—exhausted, covered in sweat and sawdust, but we're done. We stand back and look at what we've created, what we've saved, and it's perfect, it's better than perfect, it's ours.

Dave returns at six, checks the work, nods. "Looks good," he says. "You pass."

I nearly cry with relief, but I hold it together because tonight is about celebration, about showing this town what we've built, what we've saved.

West looks at me, and there's something in his eyes, something like pride, like wonder, like he's seeing me for the first time, really seeing me. "We did it," he says.

"We did," I agree, and the words feel like a promise, like a beginning.

Today's Playlist:
"Roof Dare" – Morning Electric
"Italian Law Cannoli" – Celebration Requirements
"Two Degrees and a Dream" – Deadline Victory

Day 9 — West

The inn at night, dressed for its own party, looks like it finally remembers it's beautiful. Strings of lights cascade down the staircase like they're trying to catch stars, the rooms glow with the warmth of secrets and possibilities, and somewhere a playlist is playing—her playlist, of course—something soft and hopeful that sounds like the future if the future were brave enough to show up.

I'm by the front door playing reluctant bouncer, which is ridiculous because I'm just standing here while people who've known Luna her whole life stream in like water finding its way home. They bring casseroles and wine and the kind of easy gossip that feels like a hug, like this town has been waiting for this moment as long as we have.

Nonna holds court near the entrance like a queen receiving her subjects, accepting compliments with the gracious dignity of someone who knew this day would come, who never doubted for a second that this place would rise again.

Kelsey appears beside me with two glasses of something that looks expensive and dangerous. "You look like you're guarding the place from happiness," she says, like she can read my mind.

"Just making sure everyone stays hydrated," I deadpan, because anything else feels too vulnerable, too honest.

The party is in full swing when Luna finds me, her eyes bright with excitement and something else - mischief, maybe. "You need to see something," she says, grabbing my hand and pulling me away from my reluctant bouncer duties.

"We're not supposed to leave the party," I protest, but I'm following her anyway. I always follow her.

"This is more important," she says, leading me upstairs to the room we've been working on all week - Room 12, the one at the end of the hall with the best ocean view.

The room is mostly finished now - painted in a soft blue that reminds me of the sky just before sunset, furniture arranged, floors gleaming. But Luna heads straight for the fireplace, the one we've been restoring piece by painstaking piece.

"I found this," she says, kneeling in front of the hearth. "When I was cleaning the brickwork."

She points to a loose brick near the back of the fireplace. "I think it's another hiding place. Like the carriage house."

I kneel beside her, my heart starting to beat faster. The inn keeps giving us these gifts, these pieces of history that connect us to the people who loved this place before us.

Together, we work the brick loose. Behind it is a small metal box, similar to the one Luna found in the carriage house but different. This one is heavier, more ornate, with intricate designs etched into the lid.

"Wow," I breathe. "This is..."

"This is my grandparents'," Luna says, her voice trembling slightly. "I can feel it."

We carry the box to the small sitting area in the room, setting it on the coffee table between us. For a moment, we just look at it, this artifact from another time, this piece of the story we've been trying to understand.

"Open it," I say gently.

Luna's hands shake as she works the latch. The box opens with a soft creak, revealing not letters like the carriage house box, but something entirely different.

Inside, nestled in velvet lining, are dozens of small objects, each one carefully preserved. A dried flower pressed between glass. A ticket stub from what looks like a dance. A small, carved wooden bird. And at the bottom, a leather-bound journal.

"These are their memories," Luna whispers, picking up the carved bird. "This was my grandfather's. He carved it for my grandmother on their first anniversary."

She opens the journal, and the pages are filled with her grandfather's handwriting - neat, precise, full of love and observations about the inn, about the town, about the woman who was his entire world.

"September 14, 1946," Luna reads aloud. "'Today a couple stayed in Room 7. They're on their honeymoon. The young man plays guitar, and his wife sings along. Sometimes I think this inn doesn't just provide shelter - it collects memories. Each person who stays here leaves a piece of their story behind, and somehow, the building holds all of them.'"

She flips through more pages, reading snippets about guests, about renovations, about the small moments that made up their life together. Then she stops on a page near the end, and her breath catches.

"What is it?" I ask.

"December 21, 1978," she reads, her voice thick with emotion. "'Luna was born today. Six pounds, two ounces, ten fingers, ten toes, and a pair of lungs that could wake the dead. Her mother is tired but happy. Our granddaughter. I look at her and I see generations of love, all the people who came before us, all the stories that led to this moment. I wonder what stories she'll tell, what memories she'll create, what pieces of her heart she'll leave in this place.'"

Luna looks up at me, tears streaming down her face. "He wrote about me."

"He knew you'd be special," I say, taking her hand.

She keeps reading, finding entries about the inn's history, about guests who fell in love here, about the way the building seemed to have a life of its own. Then she finds the last entry, dated just a week before her grandfather died.

"July 3, 1980," she reads. "'The doctor says I don't have much time. I'm not afraid of dying, but I am afraid of leaving this place. This inn has been my life's work, my legacy. But it's more than that. It's a home for stories, a place where people come to find themselves or each other or sometimes both. I hope my granddaughter understands that one day.

I hope she knows that this place isn't just wood and plaster - it's magic. And magic is worth fighting for.'"

Luna closes the journal gently, like it's the most precious thing in the world. "Magic," she whispers. "That's what this place is."

"It always has been," I say softly.

She looks around the room, at the fireplace where we found the box, at the ocean view beyond the windows, at the space we've been bringing back to life together. "I think we're part of the magic now," she says. "Our story is going to be one of the ones this place holds."

I pull her into my arms, holding her close as the sounds of the party float up from downstairs. "I love you," I whisper against her hair.

"I love you too," she says, and it feels like the most natural thing in the world, like the words have been waiting there for years, waiting for us to be ready to hear them.

We sit there for a long time, surrounded by the memories of her grandparents, by the evidence of their love story, by the proof that this place has always been about more than just providing shelter. It's about connection, about community, about the kind of magic that happens when people open their hearts to each other.

"You know," Luna says finally, "when Nonna first gave me that thirty-day schedule, I thought it was her way of trying to fix me."

"And now?"

"Now I think it was her way of bringing me home," she says. "Not just to this place, but to myself. To us."

The party downstairs continues, but up here in Room 12, it's just the two of us, surrounded by history, wrapped in the magic of this place, finally understanding that we've been part of each other's stories all along.

Today's Playlist: "Magic" by Pilot, "The Story" by Brandi Carlile, "Home" by Edward Sharpe & The Magnetic Zeros

She hands me a glass. "And by hydrated you mean emotionally constipated and terrified that Luna's going to succeed without you realizing you've already decided to stay."

I choke on the wine. "What?"

"You've been talking to Luis, haven't you?" she asks, and there's laughter in her voice like she's known all along, like she and everyone else has been watching this slow-motion car crash of a romance develop in real time. "He called Brenda. Brenda told me. Small town, West. We have better gossip networks than the CIA."

I don't have an answer for that, because she's right, because I have been talking to Luis, because I did send that text last night turning down the Seattle job, because I'm staying even though I haven't found the courage to tell Luna, to tell myself, to make it real.

"So," Kelsey says, nudging my shoulder like we're friends now, like she's decided I'm worthy despite my best efforts to remain emotionally unavailable. "When are you going to tell her?"

"When the inspection is passed," I say, because it's the first excuse I can think of.

She nods like she understands, like she knows I'm afraid, like she knows that sometimes you need a deadline to give you courage. "Fair enough. But don't wait too long. This town loves a good romance, but we love happy endings more."

She disappears into the crowd, leaving me alone with my wine and my cowardice and the growing realization that I'm in way over my head and don't want to be saved.

Then I see her—Luna, standing by the fireplace, surrounded by well-wishers, laughing at something someone said, looking so beautiful it makes my chest ache. She's wearing a dress that matches her eyes, and her hair is down, and she's glowing like she's been plugged into the same electrical current that's been running between us for weeks.

She catches my eye across the room, and the smile she gives me is like a promise, like a welcome, like she's been waiting for me to notice her properly. I excuse myself from my door-guarding duties and make my way through the crowd like a man drawn to light, like a ship finding its way home.

"You clean up okay," I say, because it's the first thing that comes to mind, because anything else would reveal too much.

"You don't look half bad yourself," she counters, and her eyes are bright with mischief and something else, something deeper, something that looks like she's seeing me, really seeing me, for the first time.

We stand there for a moment, surrounded by the noise of the party but caught in our own bubble of silence, of possibility, of all the things we're not saying.

"You know," she says softly, like she's sharing a secret, like she's testing the waters, "the bank called. They saw the inspection report. They approved the next installment."

I let out a breath I didn't realize I was holding. "Luna, that's—"

"Amazing?" she asks, and her smile is like sunrise, like it's lighting up the whole room. "I know. We did it."

"We did," I agree, and the words feel like more than just a statement about the inn, about the renovation. They feel like a promise about us.

The bank rep arrives halfway through the evening—a woman named Sarah who looks like she's never seen a renovation that didn't terrify her, like she's been sent here to verify that our dreams actually exist, that they're not just something we made up out of desperation and hope.

She moves through the rooms with the critical eye of someone who measures success in spreadsheets, in ROI, in things that can be quantified and analyzed and assigned a monetary value. But then she gets to the roof deck, and she stops, and she just looks at the view, at the lights, at the way we've captured the ocean like it's a painting we created just for her.

"Wow," she says, and it's the most genuine thing I've heard all night. "This is... this is special."

Luna looks at me, and there are tears in her eyes, but they're happy tears, the kind that come from realizing your dreams are real, from knowing that you've actually done it, you've actually saved something worth saving.

"It is," Luna says, and she's looking at me when she says it, like she's talking about more than just the inn, like she's talking about us.

Later, when the party winds down and the guests have left, we stand on the roof deck together, the lights twinkling around us like stars that decided to visit Earth for the night.

"You did it," I say, because someone has to say it, because someone needs to acknowledge what she's accomplished.

"We did it," she corrects, and her voice is soft, like she's inviting me to stay, like she's asking me to be part of this future she's building.

"I have something to tell you," I says, and my heart is pounding like it's trying to escape my chest, like it knows that this is the moment, this is the choice that changes everything.

"What?" she asks, turning to face me, and her eyes are wide with hope, with expectation, with all the possibilities stretching out before us.

"I turned down the Seattle job," I say, and the words feel like freedom, like coming home. "I'm staying."

For a second she just looks at me, like she's processing, like she's letting the words settle, like she's making sure this is real.

Then she smiles, and it's like the sun coming out after a storm, like everything that's been building between us for weeks has finally found its way to the surface.

"You're staying," she repeats, like she's testing the words, making sure they're real.

"I'm staying," I confirm, and I'm smiling too, because I can't help it, because I'm finally admitting what I've known all along.

She closes the distance between us, and when she kisses me, it's not like before—it's not hungry or desperate or uncertain. It's sure, it's steady, it's like coming home.

Today's Playlist:
"Reluctant Bouncer" – Emotional Constipation
"CIA Gossip Network" – Small Town Intelligence
"The View from Here" – Roof Deck Victory

Day 8 — Luna

The morning after tastes like coffee and champagne and the kind of hope that doesn't come with a warning label. I wake up on the couch with West's arm around my waist and Moose snoozing at our feet like he's guarding the last survivors of an emotional apocalypse.

The inn is quiet after last night's celebration, but it's a good quiet—the satisfied kind, like the building is finally breathing easy, like it's remembering what it feels like to be loved, to be wanted, to be home.

West shifts behind me, murmuring something in his sleep that sounds like my name, and my heart does that ridiculous fluttering thing that's been happening more and more lately, the thing that feels like I'm sixteen again instead of a grown woman who should know better than to fall for a grumpy contractor with commitment issues and a dog who's better at romance than most humans.

I slip out of his arms and pad to the kitchen, where Nonna is already up, humming something that sounds suspiciously triumphant and entirely too knowing.

"Good morning, starcrossed lover," she says, sliding a mug of coffee toward me like it's a peace offering or possibly a test to see if I'm still functioning after the emotional rollercoaster of the last twenty-four hours.

"Don't start," I warn, but I'm smiling. "We have a kissing booth mediation to prepare for."

Nonna's eyes light up. "Oh, this is going to be delicious. Brenda and Carol haven't spoken since the Great Library Book Drop of '98."

"The what?" I ask, but West walks in before she can answer.

"The Great Library Book Drop of '98," West says, helping himself to coffee. "Carol returned a book two days late. Brenda, who was head of the library fines committee at the time, insisted on charging her the

126

full five cent late fee. Carol said it was principle of the thing. They haven't spoken since."

I stare at him. "Five cents? They've been feuding for twenty-six years over a nickel?"

"This is Harbor Street," Nonna says, like that explains everything. "We hold grudges like they're precious family heirlooms."

Two hours later, we're sitting in the community center basement, which smells faintly of damp paper and decades of unresolved small-town drama. Brenda and Carol are sitting at opposite ends of a folding table, both looking like they're preparing for battle.

Brenda has brought what appears to be three-ring binder full of evidence. Carol has a stack of library books that she's arranging like defensive fortifications.

"I'm not sure we're qualified for this," I whisper to West.

"Chloe said they wouldn't trust anyone else," he whispers back. "Something about us having experience with unresolved romantic tension."

I want to disappear into the folding chair.

"Alright," Mayor Thompson begins, clapping his hands together. "We're here to resolve the kissing booth situation for the Fall Festival. Luna and West have agreed to act as mediators."

Brenda slams her binder on the table. "I'll have you know that I have run the kissing booth for seventeen years consecutively. Seventeen years! Carol thinks she can just waltz in here with her fancy library ideas and take over."

Carol adjusts her glasses. "The library could use the funds. And quite frankly, Brenda, your approach to the kissing booth is... outdated."

"Outdated?" Brenda practically shrieks. "I'll have you know my kissing booth won 'Best Fundraiser' three years in a row!"

"That was before the incident," Carol says ominously.

"What incident?" I ask.

Everyone looks at everyone else. No one wants to answer.

"The Great Lipstick Mishap of 2011," Chloe says from the corner, where she's taking notes like she's a court reporter. "Brenda used a brand of lipstick that didn't come off for three days. The high school football team looked like they'd been attacked by clowns."

West covers his mouth, but I can see he's laughing.

"It was a perfectly good lipstick!" Brenda insists. "The problem was the chapstick the boys were using. Chemical reaction!"

Carol shakes her head. "The point is, the library's approach would be more... dignified. We'd use chapstick. We'd have a theme. We'd have proper sanitation procedures."

"Proper sanitation procedures?" Brenda looks horrified. "It's a kissing booth, not surgery!"

This is when I realize we're in way over our heads. These women aren't just arguing about a charity booth. They're arguing about their identities, their roles in the community, twenty-six years of unspoken grievances all bubbling to the surface over lipstick and chapstick and five cents worth of library fines.

"Okay," I say, standing up. "Let's talk about this."

For the next hour, we navigate the minefield of their relationship. We hear about the time Brenda "accidentally" returned Carol's books to the wrong library. We hear about the time Carol "forgot" to save Brenda a copy of the new bestselling novel. We hear about twenty-six years of petty grievances and passive-aggressive warfare.

The breakthrough comes when West, in a moment of inspiration I'll never understand, says, "Why don't you both run it together?"

Silence.

Both women look at him like he's suggested they solve world hunger by holding hands and singing Kumbaya.

"Together?" Carol says finally.

"Carol would handle the literary aspects," West continues, warming to his theme. "The book-themed prizes, the reading nook setup. Brenda would handle the operational side. The logistics, the scheduling, the... lipstick selection."

Brenda considers this. "I do have excellent taste in lipstick."

"And Carol has connections with publishers," West adds. "She could probably get us signed books as prizes."

The women look at each other, really look at each other, for the first time all afternoon. There's a long silence while they consider this possibility.

"I suppose," Carol says slowly, "that my organizational skills could complement your... enthusiasm."

"And your attention to detail could balance my creative vision," Brenda counters.

They're still glaring at each other, but there's something different in their eyes now. Respect? Possibly. Grudging admiration? Definitely.

"Fine," Brenda says. "But I'm in charge of the lipstick."

"And I'm in charge of the sanitation procedures," Carol counters.

"Deal."

Mayor Thompson beams. "Crisis averted! The children will have their books!"

As we're leaving the community center, West slips his hand into mine. "You know," he says softly, "for a minute there, I thought we were going to have to arm-wrestle them."

"They're not so bad," I say. "Just... passionate."

"Like someone else I know," he says, squeezing my hand. "Someone who gets very passionate about paint colors and renovation deadlines and whether beige is an acceptable color for anything."

"Beige is never acceptable," I say firmly.

He laughs, and the sound fills the evening air like music. "I'm learning that."

Walking back to the inn, hand in hand, I realize something important. This is what I was missing in Boston. Not just the salt air and the familiar streets. I was missing this - the ridiculous drama, the community connections, the feeling of being part of something bigger than myself.

I was missing home.

Today's Playlist: "Why Can't We Be Friends" by War, "We Are Family" by Sister Sledge, "Love Shack" by The B-52's

"It's eight in the morning," I mumble into the mug. "Save the dramatics for after caffeine."

She grins, unrepentant. "The inn is saved, the bank is happy, and you finally admitted you're in love with the brooding contractor who's been mooning over you for three weeks. I think dramatics are entirely appropriate."

I choke on my coffee. "We're not—"

"Don't," she says, holding up a hand like she's stopping traffic. "Don't you dare deny it. I saw you two on the roof last night. That wasn't professional interest. That was the beginning of something beautiful."

Before I can formulate a response that's both honest and doesn't sound like I'm a teenager who just discovered romance, West appears in the doorway, looking rumpled and adorable and entirely too handsome for this early in the morning.

"Morning," he says, and his voice is still rough with sleep, with the vulnerability that only comes when someone's guard is down.

"Morning," I echo, and my cheeks are probably doing that thing where they give away all my secrets, where they broadcast my emotional state like a lighthouse in a fog.

Nonna looks between us, her expression the picture of innocent satisfaction. "I'll leave you two to whatever this is," she says, disappearing with the grace of a cat who's just caught a particularly satisfying canary. "Don't break the furniture. And if you do, at least clean it up."

We stand there in the kitchen silence, the air thick with everything that changed last night, everything that's still changing.

"So," I say, because someone has to break the silence, because the quiet is starting to feel too loud. "You're staying."

"I'm staying," he confirms, and there's something like relief in his voice, like he's been holding his breath and is finally able to exhale.

"What does that mean?" I ask, and the question hangs in the air between us, heavy with meaning, with all the possibilities we've been avoiding.

He takes a step closer, closes the distance between us until we're standing toe to toe, until I can feel the warmth radiating off him like a furnace, until I can see all the emotions swimming in his eyes—fear, hope, love, terror.

"It means I'm done running," he says, and his voice is low, rough with emotion. "It means I'm done pretending I don't want this, don't want you."

My breath catches. "West—"

"Let me finish," he says, and he takes my hand, his fingers lacing through mine like they were made to fit together, like this is something we've been moving toward since the moment we met. "I don't have all the answers. I don't know what comes next. But I know I want to find out with you."

The tears I've been holding back for three weeks finally break free, but they're not sad tears, they're happy ones, the kind that come from realizing your dreams are real, from knowing that you're not alone, that you're not the only one feeling this way.

"You are ridiculously romantic for someone who pretends to be allergic to emotions," I whisper, and he laughs, low and unsteady.

"Don't tell anyone," he says, and then he's kissing me, and it's not like before—it's not hungry or desperate or uncertain. It's sure, it's steady, it's like coming home.

When we finally break apart, Moose nudges my leg like he's reminding us that we're not alone, that he's part of this too, that he's been rooting for us from the beginning.

We spend the day in a haze of happiness and paint fumes, touching base with reality but mostly just touching each other, like we're still surprised we're allowed to, like we're making up for lost time.

Kelsey shows up midafternoon with a cake that says "You Didn't Screw It Up" in elaborate frosting, because she's Kelsey and subtlety is not her strong suit.

"You two are disgusting," she announces, surveying us where we're sitting on the porch steps, my head on his shoulder, his arm around me like he's afraid I might disappear if he lets go. "It's adorable. Also, kind of nauseating."

"We're working on it," West deadpans, but he's smiling, and I can feel it against my hair.

The afternoon passes in a blur of happy chaos—phone calls, emails, people stopping by to offer congratulations like we just won the lottery instead of just saving an old building from certain doom.

By sunset, we're exhausted but happy, sitting on the roof deck with glasses of wine and Moose stretched between us, snoring like a freight train.

"You know," I say, leaning my head against his shoulder, "thirty days ago, I thought this was going to be the worst decision of my life."

He tightens his arm around me, pulls me closer. "And now?"

"Now," I say, looking at the lights strung across the deck, at the ocean spreading out before us like a promise, at the man who's somehow become my home, "now I think it might be the best."

He kisses my forehead, and the touch is gentle, sure, like it's something we'll be doing for the rest of our lives.

"Me too," he says. "Me too."

Today's Playlist:

"Emotional Apocalypse" – Couch Survival

"Dramatic Appropriateness" – Nonna's Victory

"The Morning After and Forever" – Champagne Promises

Day 7 — West

The morning feels different—softer, like the world has finally decided to give us a break, like the universe has been watching our slow-motion train wreck of a romance and decided we deserve a happily ever after. I wake up with Luna in my arms, and for the first time in years, I don't feel the urge to run, don't feel the familiar panic that comes with staying in one place too long.

I just feel... right. Like I've been walking around with a piece missing and didn't realize it until now, until she.

The inn hums around us—not with construction noise or desperation, but with the quiet satisfaction of a job well done, with the gentle buzz of a place that remembers its purpose.

Luna stirs, blinking up at me with those eyes that have been undoing me since day one. "Morning," she murmurs, and her voice is still thick with sleep, with the vulnerability that makes my chest ache.

"Morning," I echo, and I can't help it, I have to kiss her, have to start the day with the taste of her lips, with the reminder that this is real, that I'm staying, that we're doing this.

Later that morning, as Luna's arranging flowers in the dining room, the inn's front door opens. I expect another tourist or maybe Nonna with more food-based emotional manipulation. Instead, a woman walks in who looks like she belongs in a magazine - expensive clothes, perfect hair, the kind of polished confidence that speaks of successful careers and city lives.

"Luna?" the woman calls, and her voice is familiar somehow.

Luna looks up, and her face goes through a series of emotions I can't quite follow - surprise, joy, then something like apprehension. "Sarah? What are you doing here?"

Sarah crosses the dining room in long, confident strides, pulling Luna into a hug that looks genuine but also somehow performative. "I

133

was in the area for work and thought I'd surprise you. God, Luna, it's been ages."

As they catch up, I gather that Sarah was Luna's best friend from college, her partner in crime during her Boston years. The one who knew Kevin, who knew about her job, who knew the version of Luna that was trying to make it in the city.

"This place is... charming," Sarah says, looking around with an expression that's trying to be polite but failing. "So rustic. Very different from your apartment in Boston."

"I like rustic," Luna says, but she sounds defensive.

"Of course you do," Sarah says quickly. "It's just... surprising. When you said you were helping with your grandmother's inn, I pictured something a little more..." She gestures vaguely. "Modern?"

"It's a historic building," I say, and my voice is colder than I intended.

Sarah finally looks at me, really looks at me, and I can see the exact moment she puts it all together. The tool belt, the sawdust on my jeans, the way I'm standing protectively near Luna. "And you must be..."

"West," I say, extending my hand. "The contractor."

"The contractor," Sarah repeats, and there's something dismissive in her tone that makes my jaw clench. "Right. Luna mentioned you."

The rest of the morning is awkward in that specific way that happens when two worlds collide. Sarah talks about Boston parties, publishing deals, mutual friends who are succeeding in ways that make Luna's small town life seem small by comparison. She doesn't mean to be cruel, I don't think, but she's painting a picture of the life Luna left behind, and with every story, Luna seems to shrink a little.

"...and Mark got promoted to senior editor," Sarah is saying. "He asked about you, actually. Said there might be an opening if you wanted to come back."

"Sarah," Luna says, her voice strained. "I'm not coming back to Boston."

"Are you sure?" Sarah looks around the inn again. "Because this seems like... a detour. Not a destination."

That's when I've had enough. "Luna built this place," I say, my voice firm. "She designed the rooms, handled the renovations, wrote the stories that brought this building back to life. She's not on a detour. She's home."

Sarah blinks, surprised by my intervention. "I didn't mean..."

"Yes, you did," Luna says quietly, and her voice holds a note of finality. "You meant to remind me of everything I'm missing. But Sarah, you're wrong. I'm not missing anything. I found what I was looking for."

She looks at me, and in her eyes, I see everything - the certainty, the peace, the love that's grown between us like the roses in Nonna's garden.

"This is my life now," Luna continues, addressing Sarah but speaking to both of us. "The salt air, the creaky floors, the ridiculous small town drama. This man who loves me even when I'm covered in paint and frustrated. This place that feels like coming home every single day."

Sarah studies her for a long moment, and something in her expression softens. "You look happy," she says, and it sounds like a genuine realization.

"I am," Luna says simply. "Happier than I've ever been."

After Sarah leaves, the inn feels quiet, but it's a comfortable quiet, like the peace that comes after a storm. Luna comes over to where I'm working on a window frame.

"Thank you," she says softly.

"For what?"

"For defending me. For seeing what I have here. For believing in this."

I stop working and take her hands. "Luna, I've been believing in us since we were seventeen. I'm not going to stop now."

She leans her head against my shoulder, and we stand there for a long time, just breathing together. "You know," she says finally, "I used to think that success meant having people envy my life. Now I know that success means loving the life you have enough that you don't care if anyone else envies it."

"That's the smartest thing I've ever heard you say," I say, and she laughs.

"I have my moments," she admits. "Especially when I'm around the right people."

"The right people?"

"You," she says simply. "You make me better, West. You make me want to be the person you already think I am."

And standing there in the inn we built together, surrounded by the life we've chosen, I realize that Sarah's visit wasn't a disruption at all. It was a confirmation. A reminder that we're exactly where we're supposed to be.

Today's Playlist: "The Story" by Brandi Carlile, "My Wish" by Rascal Flatts, "I Hope You Dance" by Lee Ann Womack

She kisses me back, slow and sweet, like we have all the time in the world, like we're not on anyone else's schedule anymore. Moose, of course, chooses this moment to insert himself between us, pawing at my hand like he's demanding his share of the affection, like he's reminding us that he's been rooting for this since day one.

"Traitor," I mutter, scratching behind his ears like the hypocrite I am.

"He's not a traitor," Luna laughs, sitting up and stretching in a way that should be illegal. "He's just efficient. He's been trying to get us together for three weeks."

We spend the morning in a haze of domestic bliss that feels both brand new and deeply familiar. Coffee on the porch while the fog burns off the bay. Nonna appears with pastries and knowing looks, like she's been orchestrating this from the beginning, like she knew we'd end up here all along.

"You two look disgustingly happy," she announces, setting down a plate of cannoli like she's rewarding good behavior. "It's about time."

By afternoon, reality starts to creep back in—emails to answer, phone calls to return, the practicalities of actually running an inn now that we've saved it. But even the administrative work feels different now, feels less like a burden and more like building something together, like we're creating a future instead of just surviving the present.

Luna's in the office with her spreadsheets and color-coded pens, looking ridiculously organized and beautiful, and I'm in the workshop going through the remaining projects, making lists of what needs to be done before the grand opening.

"You know," she says, leaning against the doorway, watching me work, "we're going to need a name."

I look up from my measuring tape. "For what?"

"The inn," she says, like it's the most obvious thing in the world. "We can't just call it 'the Castellano Inn' forever. We need something that reflects what we've built, what we've become."

I think about it for a minute, think about the journey that brought us here, about the building that saved us both, about the love that grew in the walls like ivy, like it was meant to be there all along.

"Thirty Days," I say, before I can stop myself, before I can talk myself out of it.

Her eyes light up. "What?"

"Thirty Days," I repeat, feeling like I'm admitting something important, like I'm naming the thing that changed everything. "That's what brought us here. That's what saved this place. That's what saved us."

A slow smile spreads across her face. "Thirty Days of You," she says, testing the words, trying them on for size. "I like it."

"Me too," I admit, because I do, because it feels right, like it honors the journey, like it acknowledges the deadline that became a lifeline.

The afternoon passes in a comfortable rhythm of work and conversation, of planning and dreaming. We talk about the grand opening, about marketing strategies, about whether we should keep the ugly light fixture in the hallway because it has character or replace it because it's objectively hideous.

(We keep it, because Luna argues that character is more important than aesthetics, and because I'm learning that some battles aren't worth fighting when you're this happy.)

By sunset, we're sitting on the roof deck with glasses of wine, watching the ocean turn gold and pink and purple. Moose is sprawled between us, snoring gently, a furry reminder of how far we've come.

"You know," Luna says, leaning her head against my shoulder, "a week ago, I thought I was going to lose everything. The inn, my dream, my mind."

"You didn't lose anything," I say, tightening my arm around her. "You just found better things."

"Yeah," she agrees, and her voice is soft, filled with the kind of wonder that comes from realizing your dreams are real. "I did."

We sit in comfortable silence, watching the day end, watching the stars come out one by one. The air smells like salt and possibility, like the world is full of second chances and happy endings and all the things I used to think were just stories people told themselves to make it through the night.

"I love you," I say, because the words have been building in my chest all day, because I need her to know, need to say it out loud, make it real.

She turns to look at me, and her eyes are shining with tears, but they're happy tears, the kind that come from knowing you're loved, from knowing you're not alone.

"I love you too," she says, and then she's kissing me, and it's not like any of the other kisses we've shared. This one is different—deeper, more certain, like it's sealing a promise, like it's the beginning of forever.

Moose sighs in his sleep, like he's satisfied, like he's been waiting for this moment, like he knows, just like we know, that this is it, this is home.

Today's Playlist:
"Soft Morning" – Right Place, Right Time
"Disgustingly Happy" – Domestic Bliss
"The View from Forever" – Ocean Promises

Day 6 — Luna

The morning after saying "I love you" feels like walking on clouds while simultaneously being terrified you're going to fall through the floor. I wake up to the sound of waves and the steady rhythm of West breathing beside me, and for a minute I just watch him, memorize the lines of his face, the way his hair falls across his forehead, the peaceful expression he wears only when he's asleep.

Moose, of course, is sprawled across the foot of the bed like a furry, four-legged security system who takes his job of keeping us together very seriously. He snores softly, occasionally twitching like he's chasing dream rabbits or possibly reviewing his matchmaking performance.

I slip out of bed carefully, trying not to wake either of them, and head to the kitchen where Nonna is already humming something that sounds suspiciously like wedding music. She's kneading dough with the fierce concentration of someone who's been planning this moment since before I was born.

"Morning," she says, without looking up. "You look disgustingly happy."

"I feel disgustingly happy," I admit, pouring coffee like it's a religious ritual, like I need the caffeine to ground me in this new reality where my life has somehow become a romance novel.

"You should," Nonna says, finally looking up at me. "You fought for this. You chose this."

The words hit me harder than I expect. I have been fighting, haven't I? Fighting against my own fears, fighting against the comfortable lie I'd built in Boston, fighting against the voice in my head that kept telling me I wasn't good enough for this, for him, for this life.

"I need to make a call," I say suddenly.

Nonna nods. "I figured."

I take my coffee and my phone and walk out to the beach, where the morning light is just starting to paint the sky in shades of pink and

140

gold. My hands are shaking as I dial Kevin's number. It rings four times before he answers.

"Luna? Is everything okay?"

"Everything's fine," I say, and realize I mean it. "Kevin, I'm calling because I need to say something properly."

"What is it?"

"In Boston," I start, then pause, trying to find the right words. "In Boston, I was always trying to be someone else. Someone impressive, someone successful, someone who mattered."

"You do matter," he says, and I can hear the confusion in his voice.

"Not the right way," I continue. "I was trying to matter in ways that looked good on paper. Good job, good apartment, good reputation. But I wasn't happy, Kevin. I wasn't even really living. I was performing."

"You performed fine," he says, and in that moment, I know he doesn't understand at all.

"That's the problem," I say gently. "I don't want to just be fine. I want to be happy. I want to wake up in the morning and feel like I'm exactly where I'm supposed to be. I want to paint walls and drink bad coffee and argue about beige with a man who looks at me like I'm the best thing he's ever seen."

There's a long silence on the other end of the line. "The contractor?"

"Yes," I say, and my voice is full of love. "The contractor."

"Luna, that's not you," he says, and I can hear the pity in his voice. "You're a writer. You're a city person. You're meant for bigger things than renovating some small town inn."

"Kevin," I say, and my voice is firm now, certain. "This is the biggest thing I've ever done. This is me choosing myself. This is me choosing happiness."

"You're throwing away your career," he says, and there's an edge to his voice now, anger and disbelief.

"I'm starting a new one," I counter. "I've been writing. Not the articles you wanted me to write, but my own stuff. Stories about this place, about these people, about the magic that happens when you stop trying to be who you're supposed to be and start being who you are."

"And you think that's going to work?"

"I don't know," I admit. "But for the first time in years, I'm excited to find out."

After I hang up, I stand on the beach for a long time, watching the waves come in and out. The tide is coming in, washing away the footprints from yesterday, making everything new again.

That's when I see West walking toward me, Moose trotting happily at his side. He's holding two mugs of coffee, and he's smiling that soft, uncertain smile that still makes my heart do ridiculous things.

"Everything okay?" he asks, handing me a mug.

"Everything's perfect," I say, and it's the truest thing I've ever said.

We walk along the water's edge, not saying anything, just comfortable in the silence that's settled between us. Moose chases seagulls with the joyful enthusiasm of a dog who knows he's found his forever home.

"You know," West says after a while, "I was thinking about what you said before. About finding your way back to yourself."

I squeeze his hand. "And?"

"I think that's what this inn is," he says, looking at the building that's been the backdrop to both our childhoods and our reunion. "It's not just wood and plaster and memories. It's a place where people find themselves again."

"Like your grandfather?"

"Like you," he says softly. "Like me."

We stop walking and face each other, the ocean at our backs, the future ahead of us. "I was so scared to come back here," I admit. "Scared that I'd failed, scared that I'd regret leaving Boston, scared that I wasn't strong enough to build something real."

"And now?"

"Now I know that strength isn't about never being scared," I say, looking into his eyes, into the face of the man who's been quietly loving me for half my life. "It's about being scared and doing it anyway. It's about choosing the hard thing because it's the right thing."

West pulls me into his arms then, and I rest my head against his chest, listening to the steady rhythm of his heart. It feels like coming home, like all the wandering and searching and running has finally led me exactly where I need to be.

"I love you," I whisper against his shirt.

"I know," he says, and I can hear the smile in his voice. "I've always known."

The sun is higher now, painting the beach in brilliant gold. In the distance, I can hear the sounds of the town waking up - Chloe opening the bakery, Mayor Thompson heading to his office, Brenda and Carol probably arguing about something ridiculous but ultimately harmless.

This is my life now. Not the life I planned, not the life I thought I wanted, but the life I chose. The life that chose me back.

Today's Playlist: "I Choose You" by Sara Bareilles, "This Is the New Year" by A Great Big World, "Home" by Philip Phillips

Nonna stops kneading and looks at me, really looks at me. "But?"

I should have known she'd see it. I should have known that after a lifetime of reading my microexpressions and interpreting my silences, she'd know that happiness this complicated comes with complications.

"But what if this is just... the inn?" I say finally, the words coming out in a rush. "What if this feeling, this connection we have, is tied to this place? To this project? What happens when the renovation is done? When the stress is gone? When we're not working side by side every day, solving problems and making things together?"

Nonna resumes her kneading, the rhythmic motion somehow calming. "You think love is just a byproduct of construction?"

"I think intense situations create intense emotions," I say, pacing around the kitchen. "I think proximity and shared goals can feel like something deeper than they are. I spent ten years in Boston chasing professional validation, and I'm terrified I'm just chasing emotional validation now."

"Validation from West?"

"Validation from myself," I correct. "Validation that I'm not a failure. That I can actually finish something important. That I'm not just the girl who ran away from home because she was scared."

Nonna sets down her dough and wipes her hands on her apron. "Luna, sit down."

I sit, because when Nonna uses that tone, you sit.

"When your grandfather and I bought this inn," she says, her voice soft with memory, "we were scared too. We had no money, no experience, and everyone told us we were crazy. But we had each other, and we had this dream."

She takes my hand. "The first year was hell. The roof leaked, the furnace broke, we had more mice than guests. There were days I wanted to pack my bags and go back to teaching. Days I thought your grandfather was going to have a nervous breakdown."

"What changed?"

"One night, during the worst storm of the season, the power went out. We were sitting in the dark, eating cold soup by candlelight, and I started crying. Not just quiet tears, but that ugly, snotty crying that comes when you've been holding everything in for too long."

I can picture it. Nonna, who always seems so strong and together, breaking under the weight of their dreams.

"Your grandfather didn't say anything," Nonna continues. "He just held me while I cried. And when I was done, he said, 'I know this is hard. But I'd rather be cold and broke with you than warm and rich without you.'"

Tears fill my eyes. "Oh, Nonna."

"The next morning, the storm had passed. The sun came out, and the inn was still standing. A little battered, a little worse for wear, but still standing. And I realized that the inn wasn't the dream. Your grandfather was the dream. The inn was just... where we got to live the dream."

She squeezes my hand. "West isn't a construction project, Luna. He's not a validation tool or a distraction or a symptom of your fear. He's a man who's been loving you since you were seventeen years old. That's not situational. That's not proximity. That's real."

I think about West's confession on the roof. About the way he's waited for me for ten years. About the quiet strength in his eyes when he said he'd wait longer if he had to.

"But what about Boston?" I whisper. "My career, my life there..."

"Was it making you happy?" Nonna asks gently.

I want to lie. I want to say yes, that I was fulfilled and challenged and living my best life. But the truth is, I was exhausted. I was chasing deadlines that never brought satisfaction, writing articles that didn't matter to me, dating men who saw me as a career accessory rather than a partner.

"No," I admit. "It wasn't."

"Then why go back?"

"Because it's familiar," I say. "Because it's what I thought I was supposed to want. Because admitting I was wrong feels like failure."

"Luna," Nonna says, her voice full of love and exasperation, "changing your mind isn't failure. It's growth. It's learning. It's being brave enough to say 'this isn't working' and having the courage to try something else."

She stands up and returns to her dough. "Your grandfather used to say that the scariest moments in life are the ones right before you realize you're exactly where you're supposed to be."

The front door opens then, and West comes in, carrying two cups of coffee from Chloe's bakery. He looks rumpled and adorable, and my heart does that ridiculous fluttering thing that's becoming my new normal.

"I brought peace offerings," he says, handing me a cup. "Chloe said relationship talks require good coffee and possibly pastries."

"We've moved past the relationship talk phase," Nonna says cheerfully. "We're now in the 'admitting you're scared but doing it anyway' phase. Also, I accept pastries."

West looks at me, his eyes full of questions and concern. "Everything okay?"

I take his hand, interlacing our fingers. "Everything's perfect."

And for the first time, it's not just something I'm saying. It's something I believe.

Today's Playlist: "The Climb" by Miley Cyrus, "Brave" by Sara Bareilles, "Roar" by Katy Perry

"Good," she says, punching the dough with unnecessary force. "You deserve it. After all that moping and spreadsheet-making and pretending you weren't falling in love with the grumpy contractor."

I choke on my coffee. "I wasn't pretending!"

She gives me a look that says she knows everything, that she's known everything since day one, that she's been humoring me like she humors small children who think they're being sneaky about eating cookies before dinner. "Cara, you've been about as subtle as a hurricane in a teacup."

Before I can formulate a response that's both dignified and doesn't sound like I'm a teenager who just discovered romance, West appears in the doorway, looking rumpled and adorable and entirely too mine.

"Morning," he says, and his voice is still rough with sleep, with the vulnerability that makes my heart do that ridiculous fluttering thing.

Nonna looks between us, her expression the picture of innocent satisfaction. "I'll leave you two to whatever this is," she says, disappearing with the grace of a cat who's just caught a particularly satisfying canary. "Just try not to scar the permanently impressionable Moose with your adult behavior."

We stand there in the kitchen silence, the air thick with everything that's changed, everything that's still changing, everything that feels like it's been building toward this moment forever.

"So," I say, because someone has to break the silence, because the quiet is starting to feel too loud. "We said it."

"We said it," he confirms, and there's something like relief in his voice, like he's been holding his breath and is finally able to exhale.

"And?" I ask, and the question hangs in the air between us, heavy with meaning, with all the possibilities we're still exploring, all the things we're still discovering about each other.

He crosses the distance between us, wraps his arms around my waist, pulls me close until I can feel the steady beat of his heart against my palm. "And I'm not going anywhere," he says, and his voice is low, rough with emotion. "Unless you're planning on running again."

I laugh, burying my face in his chest, breathing in the scent of cedar and coffee and the man who's somehow become my home. "I think I'm done running. It seems to be your thing, not mine."

"Used to be," he corrects, kissing the top of my head. "Not anymore."

The day passes in a happy blur of final preparations for the grand opening, of small moments that feel big with significance, of touches and glances and the kind of easy intimacy that takes years to build but somehow feels like we've had it forever.

Kelsey shows up midafternoon with a bottle of champagne and the kind of knowing look that says she's been waiting for this, that she's been rooting for us even when we were too stubborn to root for ourselves.

"You two are still disgustingly happy," she announces, surveying us where we're sitting on the porch steps, my head on his shoulder, his arm around me like he's afraid I might disappear if he lets go. "It's getting worse. Pretty soon you're going to start finishing each other's sentences."

"We're working on it," West deadpans, but he's smiling, and I can feel it against my hair.

By sunset, we're on the roof deck with glasses of champagne and Moose stretched between us, watching the ocean turn shades of gold and pink and purple that don't seem real, like they're something we dreamed up.

"To us," West says, raising his glass, and his voice is thick with emotion, with all the things we've been through, all the things we've survived.

"To us," I echo, and the words feel like a promise, like the beginning of forever.

We drink, and the champagne bubbles like possibility, like all the good things that are still coming, all the dreams we're going to build together.

"You know," I say, leaning my head against his shoulder, "a month ago, I thought my life was over. I thought I'd failed at everything, that I'd lost my dream, that I'd never be happy again."

He tightens his arm around me, pulls me closer. "You didn't fail at anything, Luna. You found something better."

"Yeah," I agree, and my voice is soft, filled with the kind of wonder that comes from realizing your dreams are real. "I did."

We sit in comfortable silence, watching the day end, watching the stars come out one by one. The air smells like salt and champagne and the kind of hope that doesn't come with a warning label, the kind that feels like it might actually last.

"Thirty days," I say, thinking about how much has changed, about how much we've grown, about how different my life is now from the life I thought I was destined to live.

"Thirty days," he repeats, and there's wonder in his voice, like he's just realizing it too, like he's just understanding how much can change in such a short time.

"Who would have thought?" I ask, and it's a real question, because I certainly didn't see this coming, didn't expect to find the love of my life in a rundown coastal inn with a grumpy contractor and a matchmaking German Shepherd.

"I did," Nonna says from the doorway, and we both jump because we didn't hear her come up, didn't realize we had an audience for our moment. "I knew from day one."

She joins us on the deck, sitting beside us like she belongs here, like she's been part of this all along.

"You two," she says, looking between us with eyes that shine with love, with pride, with the satisfaction of a job well done, "were always going to find each other. It was just a matter of when."

I look at West, and he looks at me, and we're both smiling, because she's right, because this feels like it was meant to be, like we were always heading toward this moment, like all the detours and dead ends and wrong turns were just leading us here, to each other, to this.

Today's Playlist:
"Hurricane in a Teacup" – Subtle Romance
"Adult Behavior" – Moose Protection
"Thirty Days of Forever" – Champagne Dreams

Day 5 — West

The day before the grand opening feels like the deep breath before a plunge, like the moment right before the curtain rises on a play you've been rehearsing your whole life. The inn is ready—rooms painted and staged, linens crisp, decorations arranged with the kind of care that feels like love, like hope.

Luna's everywhere at once, flitting between rooms like a hummingbird on a mission, checking details with the fierce concentration of someone who knows this is her moment, this is her dream coming to life.

I'm in the workshop putting the finishing touches on the sign for the front of the building—"Thirty Days of You" carved into weathered wood, elegant and understated and somehow perfect. The letters are smooth under my fingers, and I think about how much this journey has changed me, how much she's changed me.

"Almost done?" Luna asks from the doorway, and her voice is soft, warm, like she's been standing there watching me work, like she can't stay away any more than I can.

"Just one more coat," I say, without looking up, because if I look at her, if I let myself get lost in those eyes, I'll never finish this, and this needs to be done by tonight.

That's when I hear it - a car pulling up to the inn. Not just any car, but one of those expensive sports cars that looks wildly out of place on Harbor Street. The kind of car that belongs in Boston, not here.

Luna turns toward the sound, her face confused. "Are we expecting someone?"

Before I can answer, a man gets out of the car. He's wearing a tailored suit that probably costs more than my truck, and he has that look of someone who's never worked with his hands a day in his life. He looks around the inn like he's appraising it, like he's calculating its value instead of seeing its heart.

"Luna?" he calls, and something in his voice makes my stomach clench. This isn't just anyone. This is someone from her past.

Luna's face goes white. "Kevin? What are you doing here?"

Kevin. The ex from Boston. The one who broke her heart.

"I came to see you," he says, walking toward her. "I called, but you didn't answer. Your grandmother gave me the address."

Of course she did. Nonna plays dirty when she thinks she's helping.

"Kevin, you can't just show up here," Luna says, but her voice is shaky, like she's seeing a ghost.

"Can't I?" He smiles, but it doesn't reach his eyes. "I was worried about you. You just disappeared without saying goodbye. Without finishing your article."

"The article's done," Luna says, but I can hear the lie in her voice. "I sent it in."

"Really?" Kevin raises an eyebrow. "Because your editor called me. Said they never received it. Said you were supposed to be writing about the romance of small towns, but you just... vanished."

I want to step in. I want to put myself between them. But this isn't my fight. This is her past, and she has to deal with it herself.

"Luna," Kevin says, his voice softening, "I know things ended badly between us. But I miss you. Boston misses you. Your career misses you."

"My career is fine," she says, but her voice lacks conviction.

"Is it?" He gestures around the inn. "This is... charming. Really. But is this what you want? To spend your life painting walls and fixing up some old building in a town you couldn't wait to leave?"

"She's happy here," I say, because someone needs to defend her, defend this place.

Kevin finally looks at me, really looks at me, and I can see the moment he puts it all together. The hammer in my hand, the sawdust on my clothes, the way Luna keeps glancing at me like I'm her anchor in a storm.

"And you must be the contractor," he says, his voice dripping with condescension. "The local help."

"West," I say, extending my hand. "The man who's been helping her rebuild her family's legacy."

Kevin doesn't take my hand. "Right. Well, Luna, can we talk? Alone?"

She looks between us, torn. "Kevin, I..."

"Please," he says. "Just five minutes."

Luna nods and follows him toward the beach behind the inn. I watch them go, my heart pounding with a jealousy I haven't felt since high school. I want to follow them, to hear what he's saying, to make sure he doesn't talk her out of this - out of us.

Instead, I go back to my workshop, but my hands are shaking too badly to work. I can hear their voices from the beach, muffled but clear enough to catch words like "future," "career," "mistake," "Boston."

About ten minutes later, Luna comes back alone. Her eyes are red, like she's been crying.

"He wants me to come back to Boston," she says quietly. "Says he can get my old job back. Says he made a mistake letting me go."

"And what do you want?" I ask, my voice barely above a whisper.

She looks at me, really looks at me, and I can see the war going on inside her. The pull of her old life versus the promise of this new one. The security of what she knows versus the risk of what she could have.

"I don't know," she whispers. "West, I don't know."

And just like that, the ground falls out from under me. All this time, all this work, all this building between us - and it might not be enough. Boston might still have her. Kevin might still have her.

"Luna," I start, but she holds up her hand.

"I need time," she says. "I need to think."

She walks away, leaving me alone in my workshop with a half-finished sign and a heart that's breaking all over again. The sign says "Thirty Days of You," but right now it feels like thirty days of someone else's story, not mine.

Today's Playlist: "Boston" by Augustana, "Losing My Religion" by R.E.M., "The Scientist" by Coldplay

She comes closer, leans against the workbench, watches me with the kind of gentle admiration that still takes my breath away, that still feels like something I don't deserve but am terrified of losing.

"You know," she says softly, "when I first saw this place, I thought it was a lost cause. I thought I was too."

I set down my brush, turn to face her, because this feels important, like this is a moment that needs to be acknowledged, a truth that needs to be spoken. "You were never a lost cause, Luna. You were just lost."

She smiles, slow and sweet, and it's like the sun coming out after a storm, like everything that's been building between us for weeks has finally found its way to the surface. "And you were the one who found me."

"Someone would have found you," I say, because it's true, because she's too bright, too brilliant, too amazing not to be found eventually.

"Not like you," she says, and she steps closer, closes the distance between us until we're standing toe to toe, until I can feel the warmth radiating off her like a furnace, until I can see all the love swimming in her eyes. "Not in this way. Not in this place."

I reach out, tuck a stray strand of hair behind her ear, let my fingers linger against her skin like I'm memorizing the shape of her, the feel of her, the reality of her. "This place," I say, and my voice is rough with emotion, "this place saved us both."

She leans into my touch, closes her eyes like she's savoring the moment, like she's committing it to memory. "It really did, didn't it?"

We stand there for a minute, wrapped in the workshop silence, wrapped in each other, wrapped in the knowledge that we've built something real here, something lasting.

"I love you," I say, because the words feel like they need to be said, because I need her to know, need to say it out loud, make it real again, make it real every time.

"I love you too," she whispers, and then she's kissing me, and it's not like any of the other kisses we've shared. This one is different—deeper, more certain, like it's sealing all the promises we've made, like it's the beginning of everything.

Moose, of course, chooses this moment to insert himself between us, pawing at my leg like he's demanding his share of the affection, like he's reminding us that he's been part of this from the beginning, that he's the reason we met in the first place.

"Traitor," I mutter, scratching behind his ears like the hypocrite I am.

"He's not a traitor," Luna laughs, pulling away to ruffle Moose's ears. "He's a professional. He's been planning this since day one."

The afternoon passes in a happy blur of final touches and last-minute preparations. We hang the sign above the front door, and it looks perfect, like it's always been there, like it's always been meant to be there. The sun catches the letters, makes them glow, and I feel a surge of pride, of accomplishment, of rightness.

By sunset, we're sitting on the roof deck with glasses of wine, watching the ocean turn shades of gold and pink and purple that don't seem real, like they're something we dreamed up together.

"Tomorrow," Luna says, leaning her head against my shoulder, and her voice is soft, filled with the kind of wonder that comes from realizing your dreams are real. "Tomorrow we open."

"We open," I correct, because it's not just her dream anymore, it's ours, it's our life we've built together.

She looks up at me, and her eyes are shining with tears, but they're happy tears, the kind that come from knowing you're loved, from knowing you're not alone, from knowing you've found your person.

"We open," she repeats, and the words sound like a promise, like the beginning of forever.

Moose sighs contentedly between us, like he's satisfied with a job well done, like he knows that his matchmaking days are over, that he's successfully brought us together and can now retire from his career as a romance facilitator.

The air smells like salt and wine and the kind of hope that doesn't come with a warning label, the kind that feels like it might actually last, like it might actually be real.

"You know," I say, thinking about everything that's brought us here, everything that's changed, everything that's still changing. "I never thought I'd find a home."

Luna tightens her arm around mine, pulls me closer. "You have a home," she says, and her voice is firm, certain, like she's stating a fact that cannot be disputed, like she's making me a promise that will never be broken.

"I have a home," I repeat, and the words feel like freedom, like coming home, like finally understanding what all those years of running were really about—running toward this, toward her, toward us.

We sit in comfortable silence, watching the day end, watching the stars come out one by one. The inn hums around us, alive with the energy of tomorrow, with the promise of new beginnings, with the knowledge that we've built something beautiful together, something that will last.

"Thirty days," Luna says, and her voice is soft, filled with wonder. "Who would have thought thirty days could change everything?"

"I did," I say, because it's true, because I think some part of me knew from the beginning, some part of me understood that this was different, that this was special, that this was the one that would stick.

She looks at me, and her smile is like sunrise, like it's lighting up the whole deck, like it's lighting up my whole world. "You and your secrets."

I lean in, kiss her slow and sweet, like I have all the time in the world, like tomorrow is just another day in the rest of our lives.

"Just one," I whisper against her lips. "I love you."

Today's Playlist:

"Hummingbird Mission" – Final Preparations

"Sign of Us" – Wood Carved Promises

"The Day Before Forever" – Tomorrow Dreams

Day 4 — Luna

The morning of the grand opening feels like stepping into a different reality, like walking into a dream I've been having for months but am only just now realizing is real. The inn is perfect—rooms glowing with morning light, the sign hanging above the door like a promise, the scent of coffee and hope and something new that doesn't have a name yet.

I wake up with West's arm around my waist and Moose snoring at our feet, and for a dizzy minute, I forget about everything else—about the guests who will arrive in hours, about the reservations that are already filling up, about the fact that this is really happening, this is really our life now.

"You're thinking loud," West murmurs, pulling me closer, and his voice is still rough with sleep, with the vulnerability that makes my heart do that ridiculous fluttering thing.

"Is that a thing?" I ask, rolling over to face him, memorizing the lines of his face, the way his hair falls across his forehead, the peaceful expression he wears only when he's asleep.

"It is when you're you," he says, and he's smiling, and it's the real thing, the unguarded smile that still makes my stomach flip even after all this time. "What's wrong?"

"Nothing's wrong," I say, but my heart is racing. "Everything's right. That's what's scary."

But today isn't about the inn. Today is the Fall Festival - the event we've been hearing about for weeks, the town celebration that somehow feels like a test of our relationship, like we're presenting ourselves to the community that's been waiting for this to happen since we were teenagers.

The town square is transformed when we arrive. Colorful banners crisscross between buildings, booths selling everything from apple cider to handmade crafts line the streets, and the air is filled with

157

laughter, music, and the distinctive smell of fried dough that seems to be mandatory at any small town festival.

"Well," West says, taking my hand. "Ready to face our adoring public?"

"Absolutely not," I say honestly. "But I'm here anyway."

We're immediately mobbed. Not by paparazzi or fans, but by well-meaning townspeople who have been invested in our love story longer than we have.

"There they are!" Brenda calls from her post at the information booth. "The lovebirds who saved our kissing booth!"

Carol, standing beside her with a stack of books, nods in agreement. "Your conflict resolution techniques were surprisingly effective. We've only had three minor disagreements this morning."

"Minor disagreements?" Brenda scoffs. "Carol, you questioned my choice of lipstick color again. That's a major violation of our treaty."

West leans down to whisper in my ear. "I'm starting to think we should have stayed home."

"Too late for that," I whisper back, but I'm smiling. "We're community property now."

Chloe appears with two cups of cider and a knowing expression. "So, how does it feel to be Harbor Street's favorite romance?"

"We're not a romance," I say automatically. "We're just..."

"Just what?" Chloe raises an eyebrow. "Living together? Working together? Planning a future together? Face it, Luna. You're the real deal."

Before I can respond, Nonna materializes out of nowhere, looking triumphant. "There you are! I need you both at the kissing booth immediately."

"Nonna," I protest, "we mediated the kissing booth crisis. We're not supposed to work it."

"Plans change," she says cheerfully. "Brenda and Carol have agreed to share duties, but they need backup. And honestly, everyone wants to see you two up there. It's good for tourism."

That's how we end up behind the kissing booth - a ridiculous structure decorated with hearts and flowers that looks like it was designed by someone who's never actually been kissed. Brenda has supplied approximately fifty shades of lipstick ("For variety," she insisted), and Carol has brought a selection of romance novels for people to read while waiting in line.

"This is humiliating," I mutter to West as we watch the line form.

"On the bright side," he says, trying to sound cheerful and mostly failing, "at least we're humiliating ourselves together."

The first few customers are easy - little kids who want kisses on the cheek, teenagers who are more interested in taking photos than actual kissing, elderly women who remind me of my grandmother and want to dispense relationship advice along with their donations.

But then Chloe steps up to the booth. "Okay," she says, dropping money into the collection jar. "I've been waiting for this moment since tenth grade."

"What moment?" I ask nervously.

"The moment I get to see if all that pining you did in high school paid off," she says, and before I can protest, she leans across the booth and kisses West on the cheek.

"Chloe!" I practically shriek.

"Testing," she says, wiping lipstick off his face. "Purely scientific. Now you."

"She wants me to kiss you," West says, looking completely overwhelmed.

"I gathered that," I say dryly.

"Come on," Chloe wheedles. "It's for charity! For the children! For the library!"

Fine. I lean across the booth and kiss West on the cheek. It's supposed to be quick and innocent, but the moment my lips touch his skin, something happens. The air shifts, electricity crackles, and suddenly this doesn't feel like a joke anymore.

When I pull back, West is staring at me with an expression I can't quite read. Something between shock and hope and the same overwhelming emotion I'm feeling.

"Well," Chloe says, looking between us. "That's not just for charity."

The rest of the afternoon passes in a blur of faces and laughter and the constant awareness of West beside me. We work together like we've been doing this forever, passing out kisses (mostly on cheeks, with the occasional dramatic lip print from teenagers), taking money, and generally acting like the small town power couple everyone seems to think we are.

By late afternoon, the sun is starting to set and the crowd is thinning out. Mayor Thompson makes a speech about community spirit, Brenda and Carol present us with a plaque for "Outstanding Mediation Services," and Nonna looks so proud she might actually explode.

"We did it," West says as we're finally leaving the booth. "We survived."

"We more than survived," I say, looking around at the festival, at this town that's somehow become my home again. "We fit in."

West takes my hand, and his fingers lace through mine like they were made to be there. "You always fit in, Luna. You just had to realize it."

As we walk through the festival, hand in hand, people wave and smile and call out to us. The baker gives us free pastries, the librarian recommends books she thinks we'll both like, and even Old Man Henderson, who hasn't spoken to anyone since his prize-winning pumpkin incident in 2019, nods in our direction.

This is what I was missing in Boston. Not just the man beside me, not just the familiar streets, not just the smell of the ocean. I was missing this - the feeling of belonging somewhere so completely that they'd throw a festival to celebrate your love story.

"You know," I say, leaning my head against West's shoulder as we watch the fireworks start, "I used to think love was supposed to be dramatic and complicated and life-changing."

"And now?"

"Now I think it's supposed to be this," I say, and my voice is thick with emotion. "Hand in hand at a small town festival, surrounded by people who've known you forever, watching fireworks and feeling like you're exactly where you're supposed to be."

West kisses the top of my head. "That's the best kind of love story."

The fireworks explode overhead, painting the sky in brilliant colors. But the most beautiful thing I can see is the future stretching out in front of us, full of festivals and inn renovations and quiet moments like this, full of all the small, perfect pieces that add up to everything.

Today's Playlist: "Firework" by Katy Perry, "Small Town" by John Mellencamp, "Celebration" by Kool & The Gang

"Nothing," I say, because it's true, because for the first time in months, nothing is wrong. "Everything's right."

He leans in, kisses me slow and sweet, like we have all the time in the world, like this is just another morning in the rest of our lives. "Then why are you awake at dawn worrying?"

"I'm not worrying," I protest, but I am, a little, because this is big, this is everything, this is the culmination of all the dreams and nightmares and sleepless nights that brought us here. "I'm just... processing."

He runs his fingers through my hair, gentle, soothing, like he knows exactly what I need, like he's learned all my tells, all my vulnerabilities, all the ways I try to hide behind confidence and spreadsheets. "You're going to be amazing today."

"We're going to be amazing today," I correct, because it's not just me anymore, it's us, it's our life we've built together.

"WE'RE going to be amazing today," he agrees, and there's pride in his voice, like he's proud of us, of what we've created, of what we've survived.

Moose, of course, chooses this moment to insert himself between us, pawing at my hand like he's demanding his share of the morning affection, like he's reminding us that he's part of this too, that he's been part of this from the beginning.

"Your dog is a morning person," I mutter, scratching behind his ears like the hypocrite I am.

"He's efficient," West deadpans, but he's smiling, because Moose is ours now, part of this strange, wonderful family we've built.

By eight, the inn is alive with the energy of opening day. Nonna's in the kitchen, humming something that sounds suspiciously triumphant and entirely too knowing, orchestrating a small army of helpers who are setting up the breakfast buffet with the kind of precision that comes from years of experience and a deep love of feeding people.

Kelsey arrives with a clipboard and the kind of manic energy that comes from being way too invested in her friends' romantic and professional success. "You two look disgustingly happy," she announces, surveying us where we're standing in the lobby, hands clasped, like we're bracing ourselves for impact.

"We're practicing," West deadpans, and I can feel the laugh rumbling in his chest.

"Good," Kelsey says, tapping her clipboard like she's conducting an orchestra of chaos. "Because you're going to need it. The reservations list is full, the gossip network has been working overtime, and I think half the town showed up just to see if you're really together."

The first guests arrive at nine sharp—an elderly couple from Boston who look like they've been traveling their whole lives, like they have stories in their wrinkles and wisdom in their eyes. They check in with the kind of gentle curiosity that feels like they're not just looking for a place to sleep, but for a place to belong.

"Welcome to Thirty Days of You," I say, and the name feels right on my tongue, feels like I've been saying it forever.

"What a lovely name," the woman says, and her husband nods in agreement. "There must be a story behind it."

"There is," West says, and he takes my hand, laces his fingers through mine like he's staking a claim, like he's making a statement. "But it's a long one."

"Good," the man says, smiling like he knows exactly what that means. "We have time."

The day passes in a happy blur of check-ins and tours, of stories and laughter, of the kind of easy intimacy that comes from sharing something you've built with something you love. Guests wander through the inn like they're discovering a secret, like they're finding something they didn't know they were looking for.

By sunset, we're sitting on the roof deck with a glass of wine, watching the ocean turn shades of gold and pink and purple that don't seem real, like they're something we dreamed up together. The inn hums around us, alive with the sounds of happy guests, with the satisfaction of a dream realized, with the knowledge that we've built something beautiful, something lasting.

"You know," West says, leaning his head against mine, and his voice is soft, filled with the kind of wonder that comes from realizing your dreams are real. "I never thought I'd be here. I never thought I'd have this."

"Have what?" I ask, though I think I know, though I hope I know.

"This," he says, and he gestures around us—at the inn, at the guests, at the life we've built together. "Home. Family. You."

My heart does that ridiculous fluttering thing, the one that feels like it might fly right out of my chest, the one that feels like it might burst with all the happiness I'm holding inside.

"You have a home," I say, echoing the words he said to me what feels like a lifetime ago, echoing the promise that changed everything. "You have a family. You have me."

"I love you," he says, because he needs to, because I need to hear it, because some things need to be said out loud, need to be made real every time.

"I love you too," I whisper, and then I'm kissing him, and it's not like any of the other kisses we've shared. This one is different—deeper, more certain, like it's sealing all the promises we've made, like it's the beginning of everything that's still to come.

Moose sighs contentedly between us, like he's satisfied with a job well done, like he knows that his matchmaking days are over, that he's successfully brought us together and can now focus on his new career as inn mascot and official greeter of guests.

The air smells like salt and wine and the kind of happiness that doesn't come with a warning label, the kind that feels like it might actually last, like it might actually be real, like it might actually be ours to keep.

"Tomorrow," West says, and his voice is soft, filled with the kind of wonder that comes from realizing your life is finally, exactly what you want it to be. "And the day after that. And the day after that."

"And all the days after that," I agree, and the words feel like a promise, like the beginning of forever, like the understanding that this—this right here—is just the start of everything.

Today's Playlist:
"Different Reality" – Dream Coming True
"Morning Person Dog" – Moose Efficiency
"The First Day of Always" – Opening Day Dreams

Day 3 — West

The second day of running our inn feels different—more settled, more real, like we're finally settling into the life we've built, like this is no longer a dream we're chasing but a reality we're living. I wake up to the sound of Luna humming in the shower, to the smell of coffee and the distant rumble of the ocean, and for a moment I just lie there, absorbing it all, committing it to memory.

This is my life now. This is my home.

Moose, of course, is already at the bedroom door, tail thumping against the floorboards like a metronome counting down the seconds until I get up and feed him, like he's the real boss of this operation and we're all just living in his world.

"You're impatient," I mutter, swinging my legs out of bed and scratching behind his ears like the good, well-trained human I've apparently become.

He responds with a dramatic sigh that clearly communicates his opinion on my slow morning routine and general lack of urgency regarding his breakfast needs.

By the time I'm dressed and in the kitchen, Luna's already there, looking beautiful and business-like in a simple dress that matches her eyes, with a clipboard in one hand and a coffee mug in the other. She's focused, intense, like she's already solved three problems before breakfast, like she's been running inns her whole life.

"Morning," she says, looking up from her clipboard, and her smile is like sunrise, like it's lighting up the whole kitchen. "Sleep well?"

"Better than I have in years," I admit, because it's true, because sleeping next to her, knowing she's there, knowing this is real, has healed something I didn't even know was broken.

"Good," she says, and she crosses the kitchen to kiss me, soft and sweet, like we have all the time in the world, like this is just another morning in the rest of our lives. "Because we have a full house today, and the Hendersons want to know if we can accommodate their daughter's wedding next summer."

I blink. "Their daughter's wedding?"

"She saw the roof deck," Luna says, and there's triumph in her voice, like she can't quite believe this is real either, like she's still processing the fact that people love what we've built, that they want to be part of our story. "She said it's the most romantic place she's ever seen."

I laugh, because of course they did, of course someone would see this place and immediately think of weddings, of forever, of the kind of love stories that this inn seems to inspire. "What did you tell them?"

"I told them we'd check our calendar and get back to them," she says, and she's trying to sound professional and failing spectacularly, because her eyes are dancing with excitement, with the sheer joy of what we've created.

"And what are we going to tell them?" I ask, pulling her closer, wrapping my arms around her waist like I can't get enough of her, like I need to feel her against me to believe this is real.

"That we'd be honored," she says, and her voice is soft, filled with emotion. "That there's no place we'd rather host a wedding."

"Good," I say, kissing her forehead, breathing in the scent of her hair, the scent of home. "Because I'd like to see you in a wedding dress."

She pulls back, raises an eyebrow. "Is that a proposal, Mr. Harding?"

"Not yet," I say, and I can feel her disappointment, can feel the brief flash of hurt before I can stop it. "But it will be. When it's perfect. When you least expect it."

Her expression softens, like she understands, like she knows that I'm planning something, that I want this to be right, that I want this to be everything she deserves. "You're ridiculously romantic for someone who pretends to be allergic to emotions."

"Don't tell anyone," I say, and I'm smiling, because I can't help it, because she makes me happy in a way I never thought possible.

The day passes in a happy rhythm of inn-keeping—checking in new guests, handling requests, making sure everyone has everything they need. It's exhausting and exhilarating and everything I never knew I wanted.

By afternoon, we're sitting on the porch with glasses of lemonade, watching the boats go by, when Kelsey appears with her laptop and the kind of manic energy that means she's been working on something big.

"You're not going to believe this," she announces, plopping down beside us and opening her laptop with the dramatic flair of someone who's about to change our lives. "That travel blogger you met at the preview night? She posted her review this morning."

Luna and I exchange glances, because we remember the blogger—a young woman with sharp eyes and a notebook, who seemed genuinely interested in our story, in the inn, in what we'd built.

"What did she say?" Luna asks, and her voice is tight with nerves, with the fear that all our hard work might not be enough, that we might not be as good as we think we are.

Kelsey grins, triumphant. "She called Thirty Days of You 'the most charming inn on the East Coast,' said it was 'perfect for anyone who believes in second chances and happy endings,' and gave us five stars across the board."

I feel Luna's hand tighten on mine, feel the rush of emotion, the wave of relief and pride and pure, unadulterated joy. "Five stars?" she whispers, like she can't believe it, like she's afraid to hope too much.

"Five stars," Kelsey confirms, and she's beaming, like she's as proud as we are, like this victory is hers too. "And bookings are already pouring in. You're officially a success."

We sit there for a moment, letting it sink in, letting the reality of what we've accomplished wash over us. We did it. We really did it.

Later, when Kelsey's gone and the inn is quiet except for the distant sound of the ocean, Luna and I sit on the roof deck with a bottle of champagne, watching the sunset paint the sky in shades of gold and pink and purple.

"We did it," she says, leaning her head against my shoulder, and her voice is soft, filled with wonder.

"We did," I agree, tightening my arm around her, pulling her closer. "And this is just the beginning."

She looks up at me, and her eyes are shining with tears, but they're happy tears, the kind that come from knowing you're loved, from knowing you're not alone, from knowing you've found your person, your home, your forever.

"What are you thinking?" she asks, and her voice is soft, curious.

"That I'm the luckiest man in the world," I say, because it's true, because I am, because I found her, because I found this, because I found home.

She smiles, slow and sweet, and it's like the sun coming out after a storm, like everything that's been building between us for weeks has finally found its way to the surface. "I love you."

"I love you too," I whisper, and then I'm kissing her, and it's not like any of the other kisses we've shared. This one is different—deeper, more certain, like it's sealing all the promises we've made, like it's the beginning of everything that's still to come.

Moose sighs contentedly between us, like he's satisfied with a job well done, like he knows that his matchmaking days are over, that he's successfully brought us together and can now focus on his new career as inn mascot and official guardian of our happiness.

Tomorrow, the inn will be full again. Tomorrow, there will be more guests, more stories, more memories to make. Tomorrow, we'll continue building this life together, continue turning this dream into reality.

But tonight, tonight is just for us. Tonight is for champagne and sunsets and the kind of love that doesn't come with a warning label, the kind that feels like it might actually last, like it might actually be ours to keep.

Today's Playlist:
"Impatient Dog" – Breakfast Demands
"Wedding Dress Dreams" – Future Promises
"The Day We Knew" – Five Star Success

Day 2 — Luna

The third day of owning a successful inn feels like the universe has finally decided to reward us for all the panic and sleepless nights and questionable life choices that brought us here. I wake up to West's arm around my waist and the distant sound of the ocean, and for a minute I just lie there, absorbing the reality of this life we've built together.

The inn is humming with happy guests, the reservation book is full through summer, and Kelsey's already talking about expansion plans like we're not still in that phase where we're surprised every time someone actually wants to stay at our place.

But today is different. Today, West has been acting weird all morning—quiet, distracted, like he's planning something and failing spectacularly at pretending he's not. He keeps checking his pocket like he's afraid he's lost something important, and every time I ask what's wrong, he gets this look on his face like I've caught him with his hand in the cookie jar.

"What are you up to?" I ask, leaning against the kitchen counter while he pretends to be very interested in the coffee maker.

"Nothing," he says, but his voice is too high, too casual, like he's trying way too hard to sound normal.

"You're a terrible liar," I point out, because it's true, because for someone who's so good at hiding his emotions, he's absolutely terrible at hiding his secrets from me.

He sighs, runs a hand through his hair, and I can see the conflict in his eyes, the war between wanting to surprise me and wanting to tell me everything. "Just trust me, okay?"

"Always," I say, because I do, because he's given me no reason not to, because he's proven himself over and over again, because he's my home.

The day passes in a happy blur of inn-keeping and anticipation. Every time West looks at me, there's something in his eyes, something

170

like excitement and nerves and the kind of love that still takes my breath away, even after all this time.

By sunset, he's practically vibrating with whatever he's planning, like he can barely contain himself, like the secret is going to burst out of him if he doesn't tell me soon.

"Come with me," he says, taking my hand, and his voice is soft, serious, like this is a moment, like this is something important.

He leads me to the roof deck, where Moose is waiting with a red ribbon tied around his neck like he's been promoted to official ceremony dog. The deck is strung with lights, and there's a small table set up with champagne and what looks suspiciously like cake.

"What is all this?" I ask, and my heart is pounding like it's trying to escape my chest, like it knows what's coming before I do.

West takes both my hands, looks at me with those eyes that have been undoing me since day one. "Remember when you asked if I was proposing?" he asks, and his voice is rough with emotion.

I nod, unable to speak, unable to do anything but stare at him, at the man I love, at the life we've built together.

"I told you not yet," he continues, and he's smiling, but it's a shaky smile, like he's as nervous as I am. "I told you I'd do it when it was perfect, when you least expected it."

He drops to one knee, and my heart stops, then starts again at double speed, like it's trying to make up for lost time.

"Luna Castellano," he says, and his voice is steady now, certain, like he's been practicing this, like he's been waiting for this moment his whole life. "Thirty days ago, I thought I was just taking a job. I thought I was just fixing a building. But I was wrong. I was finding my home. I was finding you."

He pulls a small box from his pocket, opens it to reveal a simple, beautiful ring that looks exactly like something I would choose, exactly like something that represents us—understated, elegant, perfect.

"You are the best thing that ever happened to me," he says, and his voice is thick with tears, with all the love he's been holding back, with all the emotions he used to be so afraid of. "You are my home, my heart, my forever. Will you marry me?"

Tears are streaming down my face, but they're happy tears, the kind that come from knowing you're loved, from knowing you've found your person, from knowing all the struggles and the heartaches and the sleepless nights were worth it because they led you here.

"Yes," I whisper, because it's the only word I can manage, the only word that matters. "Yes, of course yes."

He slides the ring on my finger, and it fits perfectly, like it was made for me, like we were made for each other. He stands up, pulls me into his arms, and we're both crying, both laughing, both overwhelmed with the sheer, unadulterated joy of this moment.

Moose barks once, like he's approving, like he's confirming that his matchmaking skills are officially top-notch, like he's satisfied with a job well done.

"I love you," West says, and his voice is thick with emotion, with all the things we've been through, all the things we've survived, all the things we're still going to build together.

"I love you too," I whisper, and then I'm kissing him, and it's not like any of the other kisses we've shared. This one is different—deeper, more certain, like it's sealing all the promises we've made, like it's the beginning of forever.

Later, when we're curled up on the couch with Moose stretched between us, champagne glasses forgotten on the table, I look at the ring on my finger, at the man who's somehow become my entire world, at the life we've built together in just thirty days.

"Who would have thought?" I ask, thinking about how much has changed, about how different my life is now from the life I thought I was destined to live.

"I did," he says, and there's wonder in his voice, like he's just realizing it too, like he's just understanding how much can change in such a short time. "From the moment you walked back into my life."

I look at him, and my heart feels so full it might burst, like I'm holding all the happiness in the world and it's too much, too beautiful, too perfect to contain.

"You and your secrets," I say, but I'm smiling, because I wouldn't change any of it, not a single moment, not a single decision that brought us here.

He leans in, kisses me slow and sweet, like we have all the time in the world, like this is just another day in the rest of our lives.

"Just one," he whispers against my lips. "I'm going to spend the rest of my life loving you."

And I believe him, because he's already proven it, because he's already shown me what forever looks like, because he's already given me everything I never knew I was searching for.

Today's Playlist:
"Terrible Liar" – Secret Keeping
"Ceremony Dog" – Moose Promotion
"The Beginning of Always" – Perfect Proposal

Day 1 — West

The morning after I asked Luna to marry me feels like the first page of a new book, like the start of something that's going to be beautiful and complicated and absolutely worth every moment we've been through to get here. I wake up with her head on my chest, her hand resting over my heart like she's claiming it, like she's making sure it's still beating for her.

The ring on her finger catches the morning light, sends little rainbows dancing across the walls, like the universe is celebrating with us, like even the light knows that something magical has happened.

Moose is sprawled across the foot of the bed, snoring softly, a furry testament to the journey that brought us here, to the unlikely love story that started with a job posting and a German Shepherd who apparently had better romantic instincts than both of us combined.

"You're awake," Luna murmurs, and her voice is still thick with sleep, with the vulnerability that makes my chest ache.

"Just enjoying the view," I say, and I'm not talking about the sunrise, not talking about the ocean, not talking about anything but her.

She smiles and stretches like a cat, completely unselfconscious and beautiful in a way that still takes my breath away. "The view's pretty good from over here too."

We lie there for a while longer, just breathing together, just existing in this moment that feels both brand new and like we've been waiting for it our entire lives. The inn is quiet around us, but it's a good quiet - the satisfied kind of quiet that comes after a job well done, after a dream realized.

"You know," Luna says, tracing patterns on my chest, "I was thinking about Nonna's thirty-day program."

"Oh?"

"I think she was right," she says softly. "It did take me thirty days. But not to get over Kevin. It took me thirty days to get over myself. To get over the idea that I had to be someone else to be happy."

I kiss her forehead. "You were always enough, Luna."

"Not for myself," she admits. "I kept looking for validation from other people - from Kevin, from editors, from followers on social media. But I was looking in the wrong place."

"And where's the right place?"

She looks up at me, and her eyes are shining with tears and love. "Right here. With you. In this crazy, wonderful town that drives me insane but feels more like home than anywhere else I've ever been."

That's when we hear it - the sound of the front door opening, followed by Nonna's distinctive humming. She's been giving us space since last night, but apparently Nonna's version of space lasts approximately twelve hours.

"She's going to want details," I warn.

"Let her want," Luna says, but she's smiling. "I'm too happy to care."

We get dressed and head downstairs, where we find Nonna in the dining room, setting up what appears to be a celebratory breakfast spread. There are flowers on the tables, champagne on ice, and enough food to feed the entire town.

"Well," Nonna says, turning around with a smug expression that clearly says she planned this whole thing. "Look what the cat dragged in. Or rather, what the cat finally caught."

"Nonna," Luna says, but she's laughing. "You knew."

"Of course I knew," Nonna says, pouring three glasses of champagne. "I've known since you were seventeen years old and you used to practice writing 'Mrs. Luna Harding' in your notebook."

Luna's face turns bright red. "I did not!"

"You absolutely did," Nonna says cheerfully. "I found the notebook. It was very touching. You even drew little hearts around his name."

I can't help but laugh. "You did?"

"Shut up," Luna mutters, but she's smiling too. "I was a teenager."

"You were in love," Nonna corrects gently. "Sometimes that's the same thing."

The door opens again and Chloe comes in, followed by Brenda and Carol, who are apparently speaking to each other again now that their kissing booth crisis has been resolved. They're carrying more food, because in Harbor Street, any celebration is an excuse for excessive catering.

"We heard engagement!" Chloe announces, setting down a cake. "We came bearing carbs and congratulations."

"Also, we came to make sure the ring is acceptable," Brenda says, peering at Luna's hand. "Carol and I have very specific standards for bridal jewelry."

"It's tradition," Carol adds seriously. "Proper jewelry selection is crucial for marital success."

Luna looks at me like she can't believe this is her life, but she's still smiling. "The ring is perfect."

"Good," Brenda says, satisfied. "Now, about the wedding..."

"Oh no," Luna says. "We're not planning anything yet. We just got engaged yesterday."

"Nonsense," Nonna says, waving her hand dismissively. "Weddings take time to plan. We should start immediately. The spring would be lovely, don't you think? Here at the inn, of course. We'll need to order flowers, and we should talk about catering, and..."

"Nonna," I interrupt gently. "Let us enjoy being engaged for more than twelve hours before we start planning the wedding."

She sighs dramatically. "Fine. But I'm making a list anyway."

As the morning continues, more people arrive - Mayor Thompson, various town council members, people I haven't seen in years. They all come bearing food and congratulations and that distinctive Harbor Street brand of nosiness disguised as concern.

Through it all, Luna stays close to my side, her hand in mine, looking like she's finally found exactly where she belongs. And I realize that this is what I've been waiting for - not just her coming back to town, not just us getting together, but this. This community, this chaos, this feeling of being part of something bigger than ourselves.

"You know," I whisper to her during a brief moment when we're not being mobbed by well-meaning townspeople, "for someone who couldn't wait to leave this place, you seem awfully comfortable being the center of attention here."

Luna laughs, the sound bright and happy in the crowded dining room. "That's because it's different now. Before, I felt like I was performing. Now... now I just feel like I'm home."

She looks around the room at all these people who've been part of her story, part of my story, part of the complicated tapestry of life in this small town. "These people," she says softly, "they don't just know me. They see me."

"Like I see you," I say.

"Exactly," she agrees. "They see the real me, not the version I thought I was supposed to be."

Later that afternoon, when the celebrations have died down and the inn is quiet again, Luna and I sit on the porch swing, watching the sun set over the ocean. Moose is asleep at our feet, and the inn around us feels alive with possibility and promise.

"You know," Luna says, leaning her head on my shoulder, "when Nonna first gave me that thirty-day schedule, I thought it was the worst thing that ever happened to me."

"And now?"

"Now I think it was the best," she says softly. "Sometimes the things that feel like punishments are actually gifts in disguise."

The sun sinks below the horizon, painting the sky in shades of orange and pink and purple. It's beautiful, but not as beautiful as the woman sitting beside me, not as beautiful as the future that's stretching out in front of us, full of promise and possibility and love.

Thirty days ago, I was a contractor with a broken heart and a dog who was better at romance than I was. Now I'm engaged to the woman I've loved since I was seventeen, and we're standing on the threshold of everything I've ever wanted.

"Thank you," I say suddenly.

"For what?"

"For coming home," I say, and my voice is thick with emotion. "For choosing me. For making everything make sense again."

Luna lifts her head and kisses me, soft and sweet and full of all the love we've been waiting half our lives to share. "Always," she whispers against my lips. "Always."

The swing creaks gently beneath us, the ocean sings its eternal song, and in the distance, the lights of Harbor Street begin to twinkle like stars fallen to earth. This is our story, our home, our beginning.

And it's more perfect than I ever could have imagined.

Today's Playlist: "Marry You" by Bruno Mars, "Perfect" by Ed Sheeran, "All of Me" by John Legend

She smiles, slow and sweet, and it's like the sun coming out just for us, like she's lighting up the whole world. "Flatterer."

"Truth-teller," I correct, pulling her closer, burying my face in her hair, breathing in the scent of home, of the life we've built together.

By the time we make it downstairs, Nonna's already in the kitchen, humming something that sounds suspiciously like wedding music. She's making enough breakfast to feed a small army, which, given the way this town has embraced us, isn't entirely unreasonable.

"Well?" she asks, before we can even say good morning, her eyes dancing with mischief and love. "Did she say yes?"

Luna holds up her hand, and the room goes quiet for a moment, like we're all taking in the reality of this, the beauty of this moment.

Nonna actually tears up, which is something I've never seen before, something that feels like being given a gift I didn't even know I wanted. She pulls Luna into a hug that lasts way too long and not nearly long enough, then turns to me with eyes that shine with pride, with approval, with the kind of love that feels like coming home.

"You," she says, poking me in the chest like she's making a point, "are a good man, West Harding. You take care of my girl."

"I will," I say, and the words feel like a vow, like the promise I'm going to keep for the rest of my life. "Always."

The day passes in a happy blur of phone calls and celebrations, of well-wishers stopping by to offer congratulations, of the kind of joy that feels contagious, that feels like it's lighting up the whole town.

Kelsey arrives with champagne and a binder labeled "Wedding Planning Disaster Averted," because of course she does, because she's been planning this since day one, because she's apparently been running a covert operation to make sure we didn't screw up what was clearly meant to be.

"I knew it," she says, hugging both of us with enough enthusiasm to knock us over. "I knew from the moment he showed up with that dog that you two were destined for true love and eventual wedding madness."

By afternoon, the inn is buzzing with the kind of energy that comes from shared happiness, from the collective joy of a community that's watched us struggle and grow and find our way to each other.

But Luna and I steal away to the roof deck, needing a moment to ourselves, needing to breathe in the reality of this new beginning, this new chapter we're about to start together.

"I can't believe this is real," she says, leaning against me, looking at the ring on her finger like she's still processing, still trying to wrap her mind around the fact that this is actually happening.

"Believe it," I say, kissing her forehead, breathing in the scent of her hair, the scent of everything I never knew I was looking for. "This is our life now."

She turns to face me, and her eyes are shining with tears, but they're happy tears, the kind that come from knowing you're loved, from knowing you're not alone, from knowing you've found your person, your home, your forever.

"What are you thinking?" she asks, and her voice is soft, curious.

"That thirty days ago, I thought I was just taking a job," I say, and my voice is rough with emotion, with all the things we've been through, all the things we've survived. "I thought I was just going to fix a building and move on. But I was wrong. I was meant to stay. I was meant to find you."

She smiles, and it's like the sun coming out, like she's lighting up my whole world. "You know what's funny?"

"What?"

"All that time I spent worrying about the deadline, about the thirty days," she says, and her voice is soft, filled with wonder. "I thought it was a countdown to disaster. But it wasn't. It was a countdown to you."

I pull her into my arms, hold her close, try to memorize this moment, this feeling, this perfect, beautiful reality we've created together. "It was a countdown to us."

Moose appears on the roof deck, carrying a paint can in his mouth like he's reminding us of where this all started, like he's proud of the role he played in bringing us together.

"Leave it to the dog to bring the romance," Luna laughs, taking the paint can from Moose and setting it aside. "He's still the best matchmaker in this town."

"The only matchmaker in this town," I correct, because it's true, because without Moose, without that moment in the parking lot, none of this would have happened.

We stand there for a long time, watching the sunset, watching the day end, watching the beginning of forever unfold before us. The air smells like salt and possibility, like the future is wide open and beautiful and entirely ours.

"You know," I say, thinking about everything that's brought us here, everything that's changed, everything that's still changing. "I used to think that home was a place. A building. A structure."

"And now?" she asks, her voice soft.

"Now I know that home is a person," I say, and I look at her, at the woman who's changed everything, at the woman who's become my entire world. "Now I know that home is you."

She smiles, slow and sweet, and it's like the universe is giving us a gift, like the stars are aligning just for us. "Then welcome home, West Harding."

And that's exactly what it feels like—coming home, finally, to the place I've been searching for my whole life, to the person I've been looking for without even knowing it.

Tomorrow, there will be wedding planning to do, guests to check in, an inn to run. Tomorrow, there will be details and decisions and the kind of happy chaos that comes with building a life together.

But tonight, tonight is just for us. Tonight is for sunsets and promises and the kind of love that doesn't come with a warning label, the kind that feels like it might actually last, like it might actually be ours to keep.

Tonight is for the fact that thirty days wasn't a deadline at all.

It was a beginning.

Today's Playlist:

"Rainbow Walls" – Ring Light Celebration

"Wedding Madness Binder" – Kelsey's Planning

"Home Is You" – Thirty Days Beginning

Epilogue — One Year Later

The morning of our wedding dawns perfect—clear blue sky, gentle breeze, the kind of day that feels like it was ordered special, like the universe wanted to give us the best possible start to forever.

The inn looks different now—more settled, more lived-in, like it's finally comfortable in its new role as "Thirty Days of You," as a place where people come to fall in love, to heal, to find their way back to themselves. The garden we planted last spring is in full bloom, the roof deck has hosted a dozen proposals (including ours), and Moose has officially been promoted to Chief Morale Officer, complete with a tiny bandana that says "Professional Wingman."

I'm standing in what used to be the lobby, what's now the reception area, watching Luna direct the final wedding preparations with the kind of fierce joy that still takes my breath away. She's wearing a simple white dress that catches the light like it's made of starlight, her hair is loose around her shoulders, and she's laughing at something Kelsey just said, the kind of laugh that sounds like home.

"Stop staring," she says, without turning around, because she's learned to read me, to sense when I'm looking, when I'm lost in the wonder of her.

"Never," I reply, because I mean it, because I don't think I'll ever get tired of looking at her, of being with her, of this life we've built.

She turns to face me, and her smile is like sunrise, like it's lighting up the whole world. "You ready to do this?"

"I've been ready since day one," I say, and it's true, because I think some part of me knew from the moment she returned, from that first chaotic day with the paint fumes and the bad plumbing and the overwhelming certainty that this was what I'd been waiting for, that this was special, that this was the one that would stick.

Nonna appears, looking regal in a deep blue dress that matches the ocean, her eyes shining with pride and love and the satisfaction of a woman who's been planning this victory since before either of us were born.

"You look beautiful," she tells Luna, pulling her into a hug that feels like it's sealing all the years of love and support that brought us here. "You both do."

Then she turns to me, and there's something like approval in her eyes, like she's finally, completely accepted me as part of this family, part of this wild, wonderful story. "You take care of her, ragazzo."

"Always," I say, and it's the realest promise I've ever made, the one I intend to keep for the rest of my life.

The ceremony is small—just family and close friends, the people who've been part of our journey, who've watched us struggle and grow and find our way to each other. We say our vows under the oak tree in the garden, the one we planted together, the one that's taken root and grown strong like our love.

When I promise to love her forever, I mean it with every cell in my body, with every beat of my heart, with every breath I take. When she promises the same, I feel like I've finally come home, like the restless part of me that's been searching my whole life has finally found what it was looking for.

Moose, of course, serves as ring bearer, trotting down the aisle with the rings tied to his collar like he's been practicing for this his whole life, like he understands that this is his moment, his contribution to our happily ever after.

The reception is exactly what you'd expect from a wedding at Thirty Days of You—full of laughter, good food, excellent wine, and the kind of joy that feels contagious, that feels like it's lighting up the whole town.

By evening, we're sitting on the roof deck, watching the sunset paint the sky in shades of gold and pink and purple that don't seem real, like they're something we dreamed up together. The inn is quiet except for the distant sound of the ocean, the gentle hum of a place that's finally, completely home.

"You know," Luna says, leaning her head against my shoulder, her hand resting over mine like she's grounding herself, like she's reminding herself this is real. "A year ago, I thought I'd lost everything. I thought the inn was doomed, that my dream was dead, that I'd never be happy again."

I tighten my arm around her, pull her closer. "You didn't lose anything, love. You found everything."

She looks up at me, and her eyes are shining with tears, but they're happy tears, the kind that come from knowing you're loved, from knowing you're not alone, from knowing you've found your person, your home, your forever.

"Thirty days," she says, and her voice is soft, filled with wonder. "Who would have thought thirty days could change everything?"

"I did," I say, because it's true, because I think some part of me knew from the beginning, some part of me understood that this was different, that this was special, that this was the one that would stick.

She smiles, slow and sweet, and it's like the sun coming out, like she's lighting up my whole world. "You and your secrets."

I lean in, kiss her slow and sweet, like we have all the time in the world, like this is just another day in the rest of our lives.

"Just one," I whisper against her lips. "I love you."

"I love you too," she whispers back, and then she's kissing me, and it's not like any of the other kisses we've shared. This one is different—deeper, more certain, like it's sealing all the promises we've made, like it's the beginning of everything that's still to come.

Moose sighs contentedly at our feet, like he's satisfied with a job well done, like he knows that his matchmaking days are over, that he's successfully brought us together and can now focus on his new career as inn mascot and official guardian of our happiness.

Tomorrow, we'll wake up married. Tomorrow, we'll continue running this inn, continue building this life together, continue turning this dream into reality.

But tonight, tonight is just for us. Tonight is for sunsets and promises and the kind of love that doesn't come with a warning label, the kind that feels like it might actually last, like it might actually be ours to keep.

Tonight is for the fact that thirty days wasn't a deadline at all.

It was forever.

Today's Playlist:

"Chief Morale Officer" – Moose Promotion

"Professional Wingman" – Ring Bearer Dog

"Forever and Always" – Thirty Days Complete

Don't miss out!

Visit the website below and you can sign up to receive emails whenever Nessa Kallis publishes a new book. There's no charge and no obligation.

https://books2read.com/r/B-A-ZZYXE-MUAFI

BOOKS 2 READ

Connecting independent readers to independent writers.

About the Author

Nessa Kallis writes contemporary romance about second chances, small-town connections, and the kind of love that feels like coming home. Her debut novel, *Thirty Days of You*, explores what happens when life gives us unexpected opportunities to rewrite our stories—and whether we're brave enough to take them.

Nessa believes that the best love stories are built on friendship, feature characters who feel like people you'd actually want to know, and balance humor with genuine emotional depth. She's a firm believer in slow-burn romance, the power of a perfectly timed playlist, and happy endings that feel earned rather than convenient.

When she's not writing, Nessa can be found curating playlists for every possible mood and occasion, defending her position that coffee is a legitimate food group, and making a compelling case for why every romance novel should include a dog. She writes from experience that sometimes the best paths forward require looking back, that healing isn't linear, and that second chances—when we're brave enough to take them—can be even better than first ones.

Thirty Days of You grew from a simple question: What if you got a second chance with the person you never stopped thinking about? The answer became a story about renovation, redemption, and remembering that sometimes home isn't a place—it's a person.

Nessa writes for anyone who's ever felt stuck, anyone who's been afraid to start over, and anyone who believes that love is worth the risk.